Other Bella Books by Eva Indigo

Laughing Down the Moon

Acknowledgments

Since 2010, this story has been coming together. Until February 2014, it went by a different name, one that I loved for how well it fit the outcome. A tremendous thank you to Medora MacDougall, my editor, who awoke recently musing over how clever the title was and then had a shock as she realized the title gave away the entire plot. There'd be no mystery for you. Ergo a nom de plume, *Tilt-A-Whirl*, was crafted right before publishing. Thank you, Medora, for this and much more.

I also thank Minnesota's voters who stood strong in 2012 and ensured that the proposed constitutional ban on same-sex marriage didn't stand a chance. Revising the novel to reflect that and the new marriage legalities was both a thrill and a joy.

Tilt-A-Whirl

Eva Indigo

Bella
BOOKS
2014

Bella Books, Inc.
P.O. Box 10543
Tallahassee, FL 32302

Printed in the United States of America on acid-free paper.

First Bella Books Edition 2014

Editor: Medora MacDougall
Cover Designer: Linda Callaghan

ISBN: 978-1-59493-398-1

About the Author

Until recently, Eva Indigo's writing has been somewhat closeted, even though she has not. By day, Eva Indigo teaches high school students about literature and writing, but by night she reads, writes and runs—sometimes all at once.

In her recent history, she has helped to deliver lambs on the pasture; has developed a love of travel, thanks to her French wife; has earned a PhD in education out of curiosity, and has rescued several incredible companion animals. Ages ago, despite being very misplaced, she investigated the US Army from the inside out as a member of the military police. After eight years, she found that she didn't like polishing boots, would never shoot anyone, and didn't understand what the war was all about anyway.

Now Eva splits her time between the woods around her cabin and her home in Minneapolis, unless she's fortunate enough to find herself running the hills of Ceyreste, France. It's in these places that she looks forward to un-closeting many more novels.

Dedication

Tilt-A-Whirl is dedicated to anyone who has ever wondered who those people in her dreams are.

CHAPTER ONE

Horse's Ass

The day had already been long, and I knew it was about to get longer when Michael Morales walked into the lecture hall. A few remaining students packed their book bags and made plans for study groups, dinners, hookups and who knew what else as Michael's long legs ambled down the gentle incline toward my desk. I looked up at the huge wall clock behind me, hoping Michael would understand that my time was limited. The beginning of the second quarter at the university was always chaotic.

"Windler, how are ya?"

"I'm doing well, Michael. And you?"

"I'm okay," Michael responded, hopping up to make himself comfortable on my desktop. He ran his hand through his curly black hair. How was it that he still carried the scent of his cologne—a crisp lime and woods scent—at this time of day? Mine had faded before I had even started my first class. He smelled good. I smelled of static and paper.

"This is going to take a while, isn't it?" I sighed and took a seat in the front row of student chairs. I slouched low in my seat, sat up to remove the ponytail holder from the back of my head and then sank down again. I might as well get off my feet. Despite his clean forest scent, I wasn't thrilled to see my friend. I sensed a request coming on. I rubbed my forehead, right between my eyebrows, letting my glasses slide down the bridge of my nose, and pasted on a fake smile. Michael knew me well enough to not be offended.

"It might."

"What is it?"

"We have a new adjunct teaching Biology 1001 this quarter, and he needs a little guidance from you, our resident neurobiology expert and…" Michael looked up and behind me as the door creaked open and closed. The last of the students must have left.

"Look, Michael," I said, standing up so that I wasn't at as big of a disadvantage by being seated fully four feet below his eye level. He stayed planted on my desk.

"Come on, Cass, it's just a small thing. I promise."

"No." I held up my hand to cut him off. "Look, just because I am decent at understanding students doesn't mean that I should have to guide every wanna-be-a-real-professor of an adjunct that struggles in our department. The last three adjuncts I had to guide decided to leave anyway, after I had spent countless hours grooming them. I'm not going to do it." My tirade bounced off the empty lecture hall walls.

"Uh, Cass," Michael tried to get a word in, but I cut him off. I was not going to dedicate myself to training some fly-by-night adjunct who'd leave the university in less than a year *after* I spent time and energy on him. I was so tired today. Any other day Michael would have gotten a different response from me, but not today.

"No, Michael. The answer is no, I won't work with this one. If he's a horse's ass, he'll remain a horse's ass."

Someone behind me cleared his throat. Michael's face was full of bemused delight. My neck heated with a rising blush. I didn't have to turn around to know I'd be face-to-face with the new adjunct, but I turned around anyway. I was surprised by the warm, laughing face of an elderly man. His mostly salt but some pepper hair was thick and on the verge of being out of control. He had dark eyebrows that sported a few silvery white strands, not as many as his head of wild hair, and these eyebrows had arching, laughing lives of their own. Under the lively brows, his eyes were brown and infinitely intelligent.

"Good afternoon, Dr. Windler. I am the horse's ass." He held out a weathered, dry, rough hand, and I shook it. His smile showed his amusement, and one of his eyebrows was cocked like a mirthful schoolboy's. I smiled, but embarrassment prevented it from reaching my eyes.

"I'm sorry," I began.

"Dr. Arthur Pinehurst."

"I'm sorry, Dr. Pinehurst," I said.

"My dear professor, it is I who am sorry. And you may call me Art," he said with a wink. "I can't get my Moodle discussion sections to run in conjunction with the existing framework. Michael said that you knew how to set it up so it is usable."

He knew, at least, what the problem was. I was impressed. I had an immediate change of heart, and I wasn't sure if it was his endearing charm or the fact that his issue was specific and solvable.

"Can I meet you in your office at three thirty-five? I have one last class that starts in ten minutes." I didn't have anything going on after class today anyway, and setting up one's first Moodle course could be tricky. "I'd be happy to help you, despite the impression I must've given you," I added.

"Perfect! Thank you in advance," Art said, presenting his hand for shaking again. "I will see you in my office, 313A, at three thirty-five."

"See you, Windler!"

Michael hopped down from my desktop and escorted Art out of the auditorium, throwing me a smirk over his shoulder when he was halfway up the stairs. I gave him the finger and smiled broadly. I was such a dumbass. I must have sounded horribly petty to Art Pinehurst, as if my time was to be prized above everyone else's. Not a team player, that one, he was likely thinking. I pulled my reddish-brown hair back into a ponytail for class.

My students started trickling into the lecture hall in groups of twos and threes. I forgot about Art and my bad behavior as I started the lecture on triangulation of research methodologies. The students in this class were usually engaged as much as, if not more, than the students in my other classes, but today the teaching and learning dragged.

No one raised his or her hand when I opened the floor for questions. No one commented as I described the next assignment—a mixed methods research project regarding the preferred methodologies of undergrad bio students. I thought they'd value working with students who were a few years behind them in their education, and I thought they'd appreciate the humor of a research project that examined others' research methodologies, but not one student indicated that this irony even registered. I looked at the classroom clock. 2:29? That couldn't be correct. I checked my cell phone. 2:45. No wonder they were dragging. Why hadn't anyone noticed?

"It appears," I announced, "that our clock has stopped." I apologized for the second time that day, the students filed out listlessly, and I sank back into the front row seat I had sat in earlier. I rubbed my forehead. What a long day. I had planned to take care of some mundane computer work prior to helping Art Pinehurst, but it felt so good to sit. I slouched into the padded chair and closed my eyes.

I mentally ticked through the short list of things I had to attend to this evening, and then let my mind wander...

Instead of wandering to a pleasing, relaxing place, which I had hoped for, my mind took me to a two-storied, sun-blistered, weathered blue building. An artsy sign made out of two large pieces of driftwood hung beneath the upstairs windows. The top piece had the word "Sandy's" painted on it. The lower one read "Sand Bar & Café." The door of the place hung on rusty hinges that no longer held it securely shut, but rather insisted that it be pulled, pushed and propped. There was a gash in the door's screen that had existed long enough to become frayed at its edges. Bits of colorful neon glinted from the building's interior, which is where my mind next took me. The salty tang of the air outside the building was replaced with a dank, close scent of the stale beer and sharp alcohol.

The bartender was a woman who had an armful of tattoos and beautiful long blond hair. Her face was that of an angel, but the bulk of her body kept her firmly earthbound. She laughed with two women at the bar and cleaned glasses as the three amused each other with small talk. There was a group of four at one of the tables, eating fish, chips and sandwiches, and another group of three who were studying what must be a very limited menu—it was not much bigger than a postcard. The last group sported tropically colored T-shirts, crisp khaki shorts and bright white tennis shoes. Tourists? Was the draw of this eating establishment its rundown appearance? It made me think of a restaurant in Florida called "Po Folks" where you were made to feel like you were slumming but in an adventurous sort of way. My waitress there had actually been missing a front tooth.

My mind's eye focused on the backs of the women at the bar. One had long, shiny brown hair that was loose and reached almost to her waist. Behind the swinging curtain of tresses, she was checking her phone or dialing someone. The other woman, the one with coppery hair twisted up and pinned to the back of her head, was wiping her mouth, just having finished the sandwich she'd been eating. I looked at the exposed back of her thin neck. She had a glass of milk in front of her, which she drained as I watched her from behind. After setting the emptied glass on the bar, she leant back on her stool to peer at the floor, her feet trying to locate her worn-out flip-flops. Everything about this woman looked depleted. Her tank top was nearly colorless, either faded from the sun or too many washes, and it hung over her bony shoulders much like I imagined it would hang on a drying line, appearing empty inside. Her skirt was equally limp, but the faded denim still held traces of blue. Even her hair, which was a color similar to mine, looked like it had seen healthier days.

As she prepared to leave, the bartender said something to her and grabbed a paperback book from the bar's countertop. She held it out to the woman who was about to leave. It was a copy of *Tartuffe* by Moliere. Who reads *Tartuffe* anymore? The woman took the proffered book and tucked it into the back pocket of her skirt. She laughed one last time with the bartender, gave the woman seated next to her a quick peck on the cheek and turned my way. In that instant, I felt as if someone had turned a mirror toward me. I was staring at myself, only the woman looking back at me didn't seem to see me...

My eyes flew open, and my gasp echoed in the empty lecture hall. Had I fallen asleep? That woman had been *me!* Older, worn-out and as weathered as the building she had been in but with my angular face, *my* own soft green eyes.

It wasn't me. It couldn't have been. But...my nostrils still stung from the acrid scent of the bar. I rubbed my forehead, but I didn't close my eyes again. I pushed my glasses up and glanced at the clock before remembering that it had stopped. It didn't feel like more than a couple of minutes had passed, but at the same time, it seemed much later.

I jumped up, grabbed my phone, which showed the time as 3:20, and scooped up the rest of my papers and books. I jammed everything into my book bag and headed over to Art Pinehurst's office. It just *couldn't* have been me.

CHAPTER TWO

Maternal Demands

"Honestly, that's what I said, with him right there behind me! Horse's ass!" I moaned to Asha Graile, my partner, as she tried to keep a straight face. "I was the horse's ass."

"Yes, you were, but he must get it—he must know that nobody has time to do other people's work or train other people in or whatever."

Asha tried to console me. I must have corrupted her too somewhere along the way, because she spoke as if I had given her the impression that I didn't have time to help my colleagues. I promised myself to go out of my way to be a better team player from here on out. I couldn't talk about it anymore.

"Yeah," I conceded, "he probably gets it, but I need to stop being so selfish with my time."

"Oh, come on, martyr, no matter how hard you try, you can't squeeze more hours from the…" Asha's voice trailed off as I raised my hand and closed my eyes.

"I can do better," I said. Case closed.

Asha hopped up from her chair at the dining room table, threw a leg over me and sat down across my lap. I laughed.

Her short black hair caught glints of light from the dimmed chandelier, giving her bluish highlights. We hadn't eaten in the dining room for quite a while, and I was glad to be here with her now. Food seemed to taste better here, and more romance existed in this room than at the breakfast bar where we usually ate.

Our noses were centimeters away from each other. She closed the short space between us, heading for a kiss, just as the phone rang. She pulled back, but I pulled her to me and kissed her, letting her alleviate my pitiful mood. As I felt her tongue slide against my bottom lip, I heard my mother's sharp voice knife out of the ancient answering machine we still used. Wasabi, our elderly cat, bolted from the chair she'd been occupying. She raced out of the room as fast as she could.

"Jesus," I said, the passion dying at the sound of her request to call as soon as possible—it was an emergency, she said.

"An emergency," Asha murmured. "You better answer."

She removed herself from my lap and let me up to answer the call. I rounded the corner into our kitchen, and Asha followed me. We knew my mother would talk to the answering machine until I picked up. My hand wavered as I held it over the phone. What if I didn't pick it up this time?

"Hello, Mother," I said, clicking the old machine off. I hopped up onto the counter and leaned my shoulders back into the cupboards behind me. I kept my eyes on Asha as she leaned back against the counter. Her hips jutted out in her tailored pants, and she rested her elbows behind her between the microwave and toaster oven.

"Sweetie, I need your help!" Of course she did. The only time she called was when she needed my help.

"What is it?"

"Well, I've arranged a tremendously big to-do, a fundraiser, and the speaker canceled, and I need you to give a little speech. It's the PDOC Charity Ball, and so you'll fit right in. It'll be perfect, sweetie. It's October twenty-seventh, this Saturday night, at eight p.m. at Custer's Ballroom in Eden Prairie. Say you'll be there; it will be an absolute disaster if you can't be there!" She sounded as if she'd practiced this plea for help. I rolled my eyes at Asha. She set her lips in a grim line and raised her eyebrows at me.

"We have plans this Saturday." Asha's eyebrows rose higher. We didn't have plans. She smiled at me and shook her head.

"Sweetie, you'll just have to change them! I need you!" I heard something slam on a desk or tabletop on her end of the line. I pictured her in her home office, the one with too many oversized paintings, extravagant decorations and lush trimmings.

"What am I supposed to talk about during this speech?"

"Oh, thank you, thank you!" She took my question as a concession. I sighed. "Speak about being differently oriented, about how difficult it is, about how you've had to fight, to struggle for your basic rights," she sang into the phone, sounding triumphant that I had this perceived burden.

"Wait, Mother, I don't have a big gay struggle story." Asha stifled a laugh and jabbed at the phone several times with her index finger. Yes, my mother *was* my big gay struggle. I smiled at Asha.

"Why, you *must*, sweetie. Every differently oriented child has one. You'll do just fine."

"I'll bring Asha. She's had more of a struggle than I have," I said. Why did I egg her on so?

"Oh, no, dear, I don't think that's a good idea." Her nervous soprano titter made my eardrum ache. "She's not really representative of PDOC, now is she?" Before I could answer, she said, "I want you to be there though, at eight p.m. this Saturday, okay? Please promise me, sweetie? Just you."

"I'll be there."

I hung up the phone and pushed down the ire that rose like the aftermath of food poisoning. I made my third apology that day to Asha as I explained my mother's request, or demand. We didn't have plans, but I always felt guilty over the way my mother cut Asha out of everything. Not that there was much to cut her out of. Maybe twice a year or, tops, three times a year, my mother would need me to do some damn thing to help her keep up her social worthiness.

Being a speaker for a charity ball was, admittedly, bigger than the other things, but no less outrageous. I doubted she ever had a speaker lined up in the first place for this, her Parents of Differently Oriented Children Charity Ball. The fact that *PDOC* was the acronym was not a coincidence, as almost all of the members of PDOC were medical doctors and their spouses. My mother would not waste her time throwing charity balls unless the attendees could really fund a charity.

"Well, you will be a good speaker," Asha said from the dining room. "And it's the first big thing she's asked you for this year, isn't it? The way I see it, you've gotten off lucky." She came back into the kitchen and handed me our plates from the dinner table so I could rinse them for the dishwasher.

"I don't think so. She's so hateful! She doesn't want you there because she can't handle the real gay me or the *real* gay you."

At first I had thought my mother disliked Asha because she was Asian, but after a while I discovered it was because Asha was a lesbian and we were *together*. The fact that Asha was the owner of a successful remodeling and construction business did nothing to assuage my mother's dislike of her. I looked Asha up and down, appraising her over the top of my glasses, and Asha laughed.

She looked like a poster child for lesbianism. Her jagged, cropped black hair, men's white dress shirt, and low-slung, belted trousers gave her an edginess that I loved. Shiny wingtips finished off the look that my mother couldn't handle. Asha looked like a hardened, yet stylish, dyke, but she was ten times the pussycat that I was. The only thing that looked remotely homosexual about me was my choice of eyeglasses. And they were more librarian-lesbian than hard-core dyke. My secondhand jeans topped off with hand-me-down cropped jackets didn't really wave rainbows flags either. My style was closer to tailored vintage than it was to shabby-chic. Long story short, *Lavender* magazine probably wasn't going to put me on their cover as a fashionable representative of Twin City lesbians.

I had tried the short-haired look when I was in high school, but it didn't suit me. My copper hair, when short, made me look like one of those metal pot-scrubbers or, worse, Little Orphan Annie. I'd had long hair ever since that foray into stereotypical dykedom.

"She doesn't get it, that's all," Asha said. "Wasabi, get off the counter!" With care, Asha scooted the elderly black and white cat onto the floor. "Your mother's so wrapped up in appearances that she's threatened by anything or anyone she thinks will ruin her social standing."

"And you don't see that as a fault?" I was incredulous.

"I see it as ignorance. It sucks, but it's not really her fault. And there's nothing you can do about it, so let's get back to where we were before she called."

Asha pushed me back against the counter and resumed our kiss. How did I get so lucky? This woman was so forgiving and so understanding, it was unreal. Asha's hips pressed into mine as she leaned back to smile into my eyes. Her cheeks and lips were both reddened. I smiled back at her and undid the buttons of her shirt. One, two, three, four, five. That was exactly the number of days I had to prepare the speech. And that was the last thought I had of anything other than Asha that night.

CHAPTER THREE

Worries

The blankets pinned me down, and I was an unsuccessful Houdini in my pajama bottoms. I had a vague impression staining my mind of a sneering, handsome man holding me down on the bed. I dreamt of him, I thought. He had been telling me something, although what it was, I couldn't exactly remember. But I could still hear the gravelly threat of his voice ringing in my ears. I tried to stop picturing him, but the more I tried to forget the details of his strong, whiskered chin and dangerous, but alluring eyes, the more sharply I saw him above me. It was rare that men threatened me in my dreams, so I felt especially rattled.

I could not bear it another minute. My phone lit up the dark. It was almost three a.m. How long had I already been awake trying to feign sleep to fool my body into dozing off again? I rolled out of bed as gently as I could so as to not wake Asha. I got a drink of water, attempting to drown out my vague worries and ease the dryness in my throat. Throat relieved, anxieties not.

I realized I was feeling concerned about something else, though the ability to recall what that was lingered just out of my reach. Digging a little deeper, I decided, incredulously, that I might have been fretting about money. I had never had to worry about money before—why now? I wasn't certain that's what my unformed thoughts had been of, but I thought it had been the image of that man's face and the ache for money, just a little bit more, just enough to pay this month's rent, that had been keeping me from sleep.

That was ridiculous; I didn't even pay rent. My mortgage was firmly in check, never a financial burden, thanks to having purchased a big rundown Victorian that Asha and I had renovated on my salary from the university. We still had the basement to finish, but I was not in the least stressed about finding the cash for that.

I pulled back the curtain on the front window and looked out to assess the runability of the early morning hour. Scattered diamonds frosted the lawn. I leaned closer to the window. The streetlamp on the corner illuminated the air's suspended moisture; it appeared it would snow later. Perfect morning for a run. I dashed a note to Asha and left it in the usual place—the bathroom counter—so she wouldn't worry when she found my side of our bed cold. This was more out of habit than necessity since she knew my running habits were along the lines of wherever, whenever.

In our darkened house, I silently scouted out a clean set of running clothes, threw on shoes and tiptoed through the front door. Outdoors, I filled my lungs with the crisp, crystalline air, bent over, pressed my palms to the frozen earth in front of me and warmed up my hamstrings and lower back. It was cold for the end of October. As I stretched, my face a mere ten inches from my feet, I inspected my running shoes and realized I'd soon have to hit a runner's store for another pair. By the yellow light of the streetlamp, I noted with sadness their creases and abrasions. The white sock covering my pinky toe on my right foot was visible through the worn mesh fabric. It wasn't that I couldn't afford a new pair. It was more that I got attached to my running shoes, and I always had a hard time parting ways with things with which I had shared great thinking, planning and imagining, not to mention many miles.

I ran without a direction in mind, the streets graciously letting me make decisions at each intersection. I ran down the middle of the road. My feet made the only sounds I could hear. The city slept. Had I really been worried about money or had it merely been a dream I'd had? What I should be worried about was the speech I'd be making in a few days for my mother's charity ball. What the hell was I supposed to talk about? I really didn't have a big gay struggle to share with the audience. Would that be the theme—no struggle? Why had I not had a struggle? Asha had had one. Her mom, who had raised her on her own, had disowned Asha when she came out. For years, Asha blamed herself; she still might.

After Asha got her feet under herself enough, with the help of a neighbor family who took her in, she enrolled at the University of Minnesota—only to have something horrible happen to her there. She never told me what exactly happened, but I had the feeling it had something to do with dorm hazing or hate crimes. Regardless, Asha found her own path through building her remodeling and construction business without the luxuries of parental support or a university education. She attended the U of Life, according to me, and that was probably better than any other university.

I rounded a corner onto Nicollet Avenue. The street glowed with the yellow warmth of the windows in the row of small shops and offices. Still not a soul shared the city with me. The dim lights of the shops lit up the moisture in the air, and I ran through each hazy puff of crystalline breath like a magician appearing over and over before her audience. Her audience... my audience. My quickly advancing audience.

I spoke in front of audiences nearly every day, if overtired and stressed out students counted, but the upcoming PDOC audience had me unnerved. My runner's high was in full bloom, and my mind became a garden of ideas for the PDOC speech. I didn't want to use Asha's story for the speech because it would be voyeuristic and disrespectful, but couldn't I speak in general about what happens to most gay kids and young adults? Wasn't struggle inherent in growing up when society reminded you all along the way that you were not accepted as the norm?

Maybe I could talk about how unjust the current legalities of being homosexual were. If I were to die, Asha wouldn't get my Social Security benefits the way a man would if he were married to me. Not that we *were* married. Or would ever be able to get married if Minnesota voters decided to ban same-sex marriage when they went to the polls next month. Despite the fact that I'd paid into Social Security my entire adult life, that money would go back to the government upon my death. And that was utter—

"Whoa!" I cried out.

An uneven spot in the pavement sent me sprawling into the air, my breath catching painfully in my throat, my arms wind-milling as if to keep me safely airborne and my legs grappling for nonexistent toeholds. I landed without grace on my feet and ran out of the near fall. My first laugh was fueled with pure adrenaline, my second and third with mirth. My echoing laughter ricocheted off the building walls that surrounded me and joined my new laughter. Wonder if any city safety cameras picked up *that* move. It was a pity that no one was running with me. We could have shared the rush that comes from almost performing a face plant. I slowed down, realizing that if I did do one, it would be an awfully long limp home to get an ice pack.

The rest of my run was uneventful, and by the time Asha got out of bed, I had laid a breakfast spread on the counter that rivaled a few local brunch buffets.

"Wow! Good run?"

She eyed the apple and orange slices, the bananas that sported peanut butter dotted with raisins, the waffles hot out of the toaster oven, the eggs over easy, the pan-fried ham slices, the big bowl of oatmeal, and the bigger bowl of Halloween candy. She frowned at the impending gluttony, drawing her eyebrows together over her sleepy eyes, but I saw the undisguised glint of lust in the look she gave the waffles and ham. She had an empty plate, bowl and mug before her on the breakfast bar before I could comment, and her pajama'd chest was pressed to the counter as she reached for her first course.

"Good run," I explained unnecessarily.

"I see. Thank you."

Asha's mouth was already full, so she spoke out the side of it like a gunslinger. Skipping the eggs, waffles, oatmeal and ham, I rooted around in the Halloween candy. Halloween was next Wednesday, so I'd only make a small dent in the candy bowl. I wanted something sweet, but with a kick of salt too. M&Ms? No. Not substantial enough. Twix? No, too little for the amount of unwrapping I'd have to do. Snickers, no. Milky Way, no.

Ah, yes, there it was! An Almond Joy would hit the spot. Coconut provided just the right amount of sweet. Now what could I back it up with? Yes! A Butterfinger found its way to my mouth, followed by another Almond Joy, which was chased down by another Butterfinger. Halloween-sized candy pissed me off. I always had to eat more than three or four pieces to be satisfied. But satisfied I was becoming. One more piece before I had some oatmeal and ham. What would my last candy be?

"Really, Cass, for a scientist, you sure do eat a lot of junk." Asha's laugh distracted me from my search.

"For a scientist? What do you mean, for a scientist?"

"You know, for someone who understands nutrients and the human body," Asha said. "Here"—she handed me a bowl of oatmeal—"you need this rather than that." She tipped her head at the candy bowl.

"Thanks." I poured syrup over the top of the oatmeal in the shape of a hydrogen atom.

"Did I ever tell you that my *last* girlfriend *never* ate candy? Not once, not even one piece?" Asha quizzed me as she moved the candy bowl over to the other counter, out of my reach.

"Yeah, you told me. And then you told me that was the reason you had to break up with her. You left her crying at the dentist's office where she had just been told she had the world's most perfect teeth," I answered. "Did *I* ever tell *you*," I began, playing our old game, "that my last girlfriend never commented on my food choices?"

"Yeah, you told me," Asha countered. "You told me right before you told me that's why you broke up with her. You abandoned her in your couple's therapy office...you stormed out screaming, 'You don't even love me enough to care what I eat!'"

I tasted the oatmeal and added more syrup. Asha helped herself to another waffle and a few apple slices. We chewed thoughtfully until Asha broke the silence.

"You won. The dentist...that was good."

"Yeah," I nodded, "that was better than the therapy, although I like that I screamed."

"Okay, good." Asha smiled and we continued eating.

I almost always won. Asha tended to get too caught up in attempting to explain herself through her "my last girlfriend" comments, and I just went for the most ridiculous thing I could think of. That was how the whole game had begun, years ago, really. We had been about to begin remodeling the attic, and I had thrown a major fit over Asha piling a bunch of my clothing into a garbage bag, telling me she was taking them to Goodwill because that's where they looked like they came from in the first place. I told her that's where all my clothing came from, Goodwill or some other secondhand store. What's the point of buying new when there are so many good clothes out there needing homes?

Asha insisted that it was time for these clothes to go. I took it very personally. How could I not? They were my *clothes*. They were things I wore and enjoyed wearing. Granted, when I finally saw what items she had put in the bag I realized they really were ready to go—mostly gardening and painting gear—but by then it was too late because I had already said, "My last girlfriend never decided what clothing I wore!" Asha had dumped the bag on the floor in front of me and stormed out of the attic. Her footsteps had banged down the wooden staircase that had just been denuded of its carpeting the day before.

Later that day, I had to apologize. I told Asha that my last girlfriend rarely even looked at me long enough to notice what I was wearing, let alone long enough to decide when it was time to stop wearing something. That was the reason I ended it with her. I had wanted to break up with her via a life-sized cardboard image of me that had a little speech bubble glued to its mouth that said, "You'll never know the difference."

Asha had laughed and held me as I told her about the whole scene. She was rueful when she said she was sorry that she assumed the clothes were ready to be donated. I resisted the urge to agree that she should have checked with me. Instead I told her that it really was time for those clothes to go, and it was.

"I can't eat another bite," Asha groaned and pushed her plate away from her. She rested her pajama-clad elbow on the counter and eyed me up and down. "Where do you put it all?"

"I leave it behind me on the running path, I guess." I was beginning to feel full myself. "Hey," I said, "we have Thirsty Thursday tonight, don't we?"

"That we do," Asha replied.

"Good," I said. "It'll be nice to see what's new in everyone's lives." I forked in one last mouthful before coming around the counter to give her a sweaty good morning hug and a syrupy kiss. "Oh, speaking of lives," I murmured into Asha's shoulder as she hugged me back, "have I told you yet today that you are the great love of mine?"

CHAPTER FOUR

Thirsty Thursday

"*Bonsoir, mes amis!*" Esme's smiling brown face beamed at us. She had opened her front door so swiftly that I had felt my hair pull forward. "Come in, come in!" She grabbed Asha's arm and tugged her over the threshold into a kiss-filled embrace. As soon as Asha was free it was my turn. Both of my cheeks were anointed, the right one twice, with kisses. Esme's perfume, floral and light, made me happy to be there; it woke me up a bit.

On the drive over, I had almost fallen asleep while listening to Asha talk quietly about one of her colleague's ideas for a dog park café. I had been dreamily wondering about what the city could offer to cat owners to even the score. I was nodding off, I think, as I pictured a cat park where the felines ignored each other as they perched on branches or carpet-covered jungle gyms. Of course, there'd be one or two oddball cats who demanded attention by weaving intricate patterns between the humans' ankles, but every other cat would just go on pretending to be bored to tears by life. Our Wasabi would be one of the ankle cats, thank goodness. My tiredness was the trade-off for the early morning run, I'd guessed.

"It is so good to see you!" Esme said, squeezing my upper arms and holding me at a good viewing distance. She then pulled me in for another hug.

"It's good to see you too," I laughed, and she whooshed the air out of my lungs with one last squeeze.

Esme Moreau came from Guadeloupe in the Caribbean, and on Thirsty Thursdays she pulled out all the stops with her outfits. Tonight she had on layers and layers of wonderfully bright skirts hanging at alternating lengths, a white flowing shirt that had tiny red and orange flower vines embroidered around the low neckline and, to top it all off, a madras print scarf tied into three little corners on her head.

Her brown eyes sparkled, but I felt a forced joy about her. I didn't dare ask if Elizabeth, her live-in girlfriend of almost one year, was able to join us tonight. We had never met Elizabeth, had never even seen a picture of her and had started to resent her for not coming around. Asha claimed, to me alone, that it was now past the point of Elizabeth even being able to gracefully join us—she had already turned the group down eleven times in as many months.

"Hey, Es, is Elizabeth here tonight?" Asha dared to ask.

"No, no," Esme said in her drawling French island accent. "Elizabeth has a phone conference tonight, so she stayed at work for it. Too noisy here, she's sure." Her smile didn't falter, but Esme took a deep breath and filtered a big sigh through her teeth.

"Esme—" I began.

"Maybe next time, she says."

"That'll be the big one," Asha said, nodding. "The Beaujolais Nouveau!"

"That would be a good one for Elizabeth's first," I consoled.

"Yes—" Esme was cut off by hollering from further within her home.

"Hey!" Jenn's voice catapulted itself at us from the living room, "Hey, you guys are here!" Seconds later, Jenn was running and sliding at us, polishing Esme's wooden floors with her thick socks. She hockey-stopped right in front of us, jumped to face us and embraced both Asha and me in one big bony hug.

"Ow!" Asha complained as my elbow got mashed against her ribs. "Jenn, leggo!" Asha was laughing, but, Christ, Jenn was strong for such a scrawny little thing.

"Oh, come fortify your delicate little selves." Jenn pranced back through the hall toward the living room. Her shoulder-length brown hair swung as she turned to look over her shoulder at us. Jenn was such a flirt. She beckoned with one finger and winked one big blue eye. "We've already opened a bottle."

"You don't say," I said. I smiled at Esme and raised my eyebrows at her.

"After you, *mes chéries*," she said, sweeping her hand out in front of her toward the living room. She closed the door behind us and followed us through the hall.

The name of our monthly Beaujolais parties, Thirsty Thursdays, made it sound as if we really put it away, consumed gallons and possibly suffered on Fridays, but in actuality it was a pretty tame affair usually. We'd been getting together once a month on a Thursday for a little over two years, and I had to admit, the first year was a bit more raucous than the following year.

There had been a few shake-ups and several breakups that first year. One shake-up came from Sunny when she decided to introduce a drinking game she'd learned way back in high school. She feared, she confessed much later, that we'd not find sitting around sipping wine exciting after a few months, so she thought we should add an element of danger. The objective of the game was to repeat lines in a poem, of sorts, without messing up any of the words. Whenever the person who was to repeat the lines messed up, she'd have to drink. The poem didn't rhyme, and it was tricky, at best. At worst, it was a slippery slope to a hangover.

It went like this: One person would say the line, "One hen." The person playing would mimic, "One hen." The first person would then say, "One hen, two ducks." The second person would repeat, "One hen, two ducks." The first person would up the ante and say, "One hen, two ducks, and three cackling geese." The second person would usually get that one uttered correctly, and the first person would then say, "One hen, two ducks, three cackling geese, and four corpulent porpoises." After four it just got crazy.

There were five limerick oysters; six pairs of Don Alfredo's favorite tweezers; seven thousand Macedonian warriors all dressed in full battle array; eight brass monkeys from the ancient, sacred, secret crypts of Egypt; nine apathetic, sympathetic, diabetic old men on roller skates with a marked propensity toward procrastination and sloth; ten lyrical, spherical, diabolical denizens of the deep who roll and stroll through the quee quay of the quivia all at the same time. Those were wilder nights of Beaujolais debauchery.

We settled down for a few months after several of us had to call in sick on Fridays following Thirsty Thursdays. We came to terms with the fact that drinking games weren't necessary nor were they now even remotely appealing. What we really showed up for was the connection of friends, the catching up and the laughter.

Another shake-up, also caused by Sunny, was her breast cancer. She nearly died that first year. For most of us, it was our first brush with close-to-home death. It inspired me, at least, to live more intentionally. It may have done the same for the others because changes were made in most of our lives.

The breakups all happened around the same time. Sunny's partner left her for fear of not being able to handle Sunny dying on her, Whitney left an unfulfilling relationship with her girlfriend of more than six years and Esme and her partner at the time decided to part ways for reasons that weren't shared with Asha or me. Jenn hadn't had any long-term relationship that I knew of, and even though she had more than her fair share of lovers, she had never brought anyone to a Thirsty Thursday. Probably because if she had, she wouldn't have been able to regale us with her exploits in the love department.

Of Jenn and the four original couples, Asha and I were the only ones who were still intact as a pair. Esme was now living with the elusive Elizabeth, Whitney was seeing a new woman named Cory who had come to the last two Thirsty Thursdays and Sunny had rebounded with her nurse from the oncology department at Methodist Hospital. Yes, rebounded with her nurse. She was named Anna, and it seemed like a match made in heaven.

Robust conversation about the upcoming vote on banning same-sex marriage was followed by catching up on each other's details. This gave way to a hush that was only marred by the sounds of us savoring food and wine. I looked to Jenn after a few moments because she was always good for a festive anecdote about her latest lover. But for the moment she was quiet. It was Whitney who broke the silence.

"So, I have a story for you all," began Whitney, who was usually more of an observer than an entertainer, "and I'm not sure you're going to believe it because I barely believe it myself."

Her face showed that she was still in a state of shock—she had that blank one-hundred-mile stare look going on. There was no trace of emotion, rather just a void where she was trying to figure out what to think about the story that she was about to tell us. Whitney held the stem of her wineglass as it sat on the table before her, and I could see her knuckles lightening and the tendons across the back of her hand tense and play under the tension with which she gripped the fragile glass stem. I didn't think she was even remotely aware of holding the glass, though, because she looked as if her mind had taken her someplace else completely.

"Go ahead, Whit, the floor is yours," Sunny encouraged.

Asha grabbed my hand under the table because she presumed, I think, Whitney was going to have bad news for us. I squeezed Asha's hand and hoped for something other than a tale of tragedy or illness. Whitney always had an air of sadness or remoteness about her, and I hoped nothing had happened to remove her even further from joy.

"This kid has been emailing me, this girl kid, well…a young woman," Whitney said.

She blinked a couple of times, and then she paused. I looked at her hair pulled back so tightly from her face. She had just had it relaxed, it appeared, so it was straight and shiny. Her brown eyes and light brown cheeks were lit from below by the candles that had burned low on the dining room table by this time of night. Her cheeks glinted as if she were perspiring and her eyes shone with welling tears.

"It's okay, Whit," Jenn said as she reached out to smooth Whitney's iron grip on the wineglass. "It's okay, we're here; we love you."

I felt tears prick at the back of my eyes even though I had no idea if what Whitney was going to tell us was sad. I hated to see her in this pensive agony. And Jenn's unaccustomed gentle seriousness hit me even harder and more sweetly than if Sunny or Esme had made the same action and said the same words. We all murmured our support and encouragement for Whitney.

"So, this girl," Whitney exhaled the words after taking a big breath. "This girl has been emailing me and asking to see me, and I don't know…" She finally lost the long-distance gaze and looked at us sitting around the table. "Let me start at the beginning," she said.

She told us of an accidental pregnancy when she was fifteen. She hadn't been able to figure out why she wasn't attracted to any of the boys she knew when all her girlfriends were losing their minds over various guys at their high school. All she wanted, she said, was to hang out with them, but her friends all decided that by the end of ninth grade, they were to have boyfriends. *That* kind of boyfriend. And Whit had panicked. She picked a guy to date, and he happened to turn out gay years later. The reporting of this to us brought a smile to her face—finally! But it was a smile of irony and not true happiness.

The boy's name was Terell, and they decided to take the biggest plunge they could to prove to themselves, she said, that they were as normal as everyone else. They had sex twice, once just to get it over with and the second time because the first time was a royal failure. Whitney's eyes were soft, and a hint of a real smile played on her lips.

"Is this about making a big confession?" Jenn asked. "Because if it is, you don't have to worry about me judging you. I've had a few guys along the way—"

"Shh, no, it's about the girl who's emailing," Anna shushed Jenn gently. I had always known Nurse Anna was a nice addition to our group.

"Oh, yeah," Jenn mused. "Sorry, go on, Whit."

"So, of course," Whitney carried on, "I got pregnant from one of those two…one of those two times." She took a deep breath and let it out in a whistle. "I got very pregnant." There was soft laughter around the table, but nothing that allowed Whitney to get off the hook by not telling us the rest of the story, so she nodded and continued.

"Even though I was proud that I had proven that I was 'normal,' I didn't really want to have a lasting tie between me and Terell. I thought a baby would be acceptable, but I couldn't see how a boyfriend was necessary," Whitney said.

"What did you do?" I asked quietly.

"I hid the pregnancy as best I could from friends and my mom, but when I started showing, it got more difficult,"

"*Ma chéri*, you poor child," Esme said. Her accent was a balm to the soul, but her words made Whitney start to cry. And that made the rest of us give in. I squeezed Asha's hand once more before releasing it to go get the box of tissues from the powder room. I set these down in the middle of the table, and a flurry of hands extracted what they needed.

"I'm so sorry, you guys," Whitney said through two big sobs. "It's so long ago…it's stupid that I still feel this way, that I still cry over it." We all assured her that no, it wasn't stupid.

"Any of us would still cry," Jenn said, wiping her nose with a soggy tissue. "Look, we are crying, and it wasn't even us!" She waved the tissue about as proof. "You keep telling us, and you just keep crying. We will too, okay?"

"Okay," Whitney tried to compose herself. "Okay. So when my mom did find out, she told me I should consider giving the baby up for adoption to a couple who could give it a better home than a fifteen-year-old and her single mom could. I think, though, that she was relieved that I had had sex—you know—with a boy. I could feel that she was relieved." Whitney went on to tell us that the adoption option was offered as a choice until her mom found out that Terell, a black kid, was the father. Then the adoption option became the choice. The *only* choice.

"The *only* choice? What was your mom's problem?" Jenn gasped.

"She said she watched me struggle with my identity from year one—being black and white. If she'd only known that was never as big a struggle as other things, but…I think in her own experience, being white and having a baby with a black man who couldn't stay in the picture, she was worried the same thing would happen to me."

"Why couldn't your dad stay in the picture?" Jenn asked.

"Pressures from my mom's family, I think, and probably low expectations for him…" Whitney mused. "I think he left because it seemed everyone expected him to leave. What choice did he have?"

"How about the choice to stay?" Sunny said.

"Doesn't sound like it was really a choice, though," Cory interjected.

"I don't know…maybe not." Sunny backed down for the time being.

"So your baby," I started, and then I corrected myself, "your child…she's emailing you?"

"Oohhh, I get it now!" Jenn exclaimed. "That's who is emailing?"

"Yes," Whitney confirmed. "She claims to be my daughter."

"What's going to happen?" Asha asked at the same time Esme cooed, "Well, *chéri*, what do you know…"

"I don't know," Whitney confessed. "I don't know what to do. Do I answer her? I know she's mine, I know. She has sent such long, pleading emails…begs me to write back…and I can't!" Whitney wailed. She put her head on her folded arms on the table and sobbed.

Asha moved Whit's wineglass toward the middle of the table so that it wouldn't get spilled, and then she began rubbing small circles over Whitney's shoulders as Jenn draped her arm around Whitney's lower back. No one said anything coherent; we just made little comforting sounds, looked at each other across the table over the heaving shoulders of our friend and tried to wrap our hearts around her.

CHAPTER FIVE

Work of Art

"Tell me, Cassie, what do you have against adjunct professors?" Art held his fork aloft and inspected the little mound of mashed potatoes at the end of it. "Do these look artificially whitened? My own mashed potatoes are never this white." He popped them in his mouth despite any misgivings about their coloration.

"Adjuncts come and go. They never seem dedicated to one university. How can you really do a good job educating people if you don't plan on staying long? And I don't have anything against the people who are adjuncts, really, just the lack of commitment they have." I took a drink of milk, noticing its unnatural whiteness. Maybe it was the lighting in the cafeteria. I realized my words might be offensive to Art, so I added, "Present party excluded, of course."

"Of course," Art laughed and patted my hand. "Of course. You know, I retired from teaching at the U of M almost fifteen years ago, but when I first started teaching here in 1965, I was dubious about the nontenure track professors too."

"So you're a professor emeritus?" I was impressed. I was changing my view on this particular adjunct professor, though not on adjuncts at large.

"Yes, I am." Art nodded. "I retired in order to travel and then decided to come back after seeing as much of the world as I desired to see."

My mouth was full of chicken cashew salad, so I could only nod, encouraging Art to continue with his story, which he did. He told me of how he had concluded after years of teaching that it was oftentimes the adjunct professors who had a more realistic view of teaching and of students. While he approved of dedicating oneself to teaching at a single institution and admired those who lived through thick and thin for their university, he sometimes wondered if he hadn't missed opportunities for growth because for the majority of his career he'd stayed firmly fixed in life at the University of Minnesota.

Before we parted so Art could teach his afternoon classes, I told him that I appreciated his perspective on adjuncts and that I'd try to open my mind a bit. He told me that there was no trying, only doing, and I had to agree.

"You know, Cassie, I worked with your father years ago. In the 1960s and early 1970s, he was one of the most renowned specialists in fertility medicine," Art said. He gave an awkward chuckle and added, "You probably know that already."

"Yes," I said. I did know that, though I hadn't known they'd worked together.

"I still remember the day they told me I'd been selected to help with his research. I mean, such an amazing mind—*and* the chance to help desperate couples conceive…" Art's voice trailed off to silence, which was followed by a nervous clearing of his throat.

He stared across the cafeteria as if taking stock of students or the number of filled tables. I followed his restless gaze for a moment, then turned back to study him.

"How is your father doing?" He continued to scan the large room, but his mind was clearly elsewhere.

"He's fine," I answered.

Art nodded, patted the corner of his mouth with a napkin and left it at that. I found it odd that he hadn't doled out one of society's usual banalities such as, "Say hi to him for me" or "He's a good man." I exited the cafeteria with this on my mind.

Soon enough, though, I was laced up like a Wild West whore—only I was in running shoes, not one of those corset contraptions, had a water bottle in my hand rather than a six-shooter and was stampeding down University Avenue. The day was warmer than the past few had been, and the street was much more populated than I was hoping for. I looked at my watch; it was 1:31. I dodged a group of suits on the corner—they were waiting for the light to give them permission to cross—and I crossed against the light just to have to pirouette around a stroller-wielding woman tied to a blur of a small dog on a leash on the opposite curb.

Mental note—stick to offhours if you want to actually enjoy the run. Well, if I wasn't going to be able to get all Zen with this run, I might as well plan out the PDOC speech that was barreling at me as quickly as I was barreling at the hot dog cart on the corner of University and Central Avenue. I edged between the folks on the sidewalk and the hot dog cart as best I could, and I still wound up getting a brisk, "Hey! Watch where you're going!" flung at me by a woman dressed heel to hat in pale pink marred only by a red blob on her shirt.

"Ketchup on your lapel," I managed to say as I zipped out of retort range. This run couldn't be over soon enough for me. I had no afternoon classes to teach today, so if I chose I could actually slow down and enjoy the human obstacles the time of day was presenting me with, but I just couldn't get in the mood. I also couldn't get my breath because I was running well beyond my normal pace just to get the run over and done with. Nothing was coming to me for the PDOC speech, so I decided to run some fartleks just to give my mind something to chew on as my legs ate up the pavement.

I picked a moving target for my first short sprint. A huge man in a gray sweatshirt and jeans a block and a half away from me. I'd run at my top speed until I got to him and then slow down a bit before picking my next fartlek goal. Okay, buddy, here I come. He was looking at his cell phone. I picked up the pace and darted down the sidewalk at my sizeable target. After half a block disappeared under my feet, he tucked his cell phone into his pocket and started walking toward me. Ah, yes! He was going to cooperate. That's right, fella, keep walking toward me because I am damn tired. Keep coming. Yes! Whew. The gray sweatshirt man and I came abreast of each other and kept going in our own directions. He was moving like a ship in the wake of others on the sidewalk, and I was slowing down like I was coming into harbor but not completely stopping to dock.

I jogged a full block, wishing I could drop some ballast over the side, before I picked my next aim. There was a small, wiry white woman two blocks down. She appeared to be wearing black spandex leggings and a peach-colored short-sleeve shirt despite the lateness in the year. Or she might be topless…making her an even more interesting finish line to sprint towards. I let my breath return, a false hope I was willing to deceive my lungs with, before I shot off down the block on my second fartlek. I'd do one more after this one and then have an easy jog back. Maybe I'd stretch at the river's edge before returning.

The woman was not topless; she was indeed wearing a peach-colored shirt. Oh well, I still ran at her the way the crazy Swedes who invented these things run toward meatballs. Was it the Swedes who invented fartleks? And did Swedes really eat meatballs? What the hell? Where did my target go? I still raced forward, but I couldn't see her. Shit. How long would I have to run…oh, there she was at the…no, no, no…there she was at the bike rack, swinging one little spandexed thigh over the saddle of her Schwinn. God damn it.

Could I make it to her before she pedaled off? If I could, my fartlek would be over. If I couldn't, I'd have to chase down my target or have an unsuccessful fartlek. Goddamn Swedes. I tucked my elbows close, put my head down, assumed every other stereotypically bad running position and bolted for the peach top. She was fiddling with something I couldn't see in front of her, straddling the bike, not yet moving. I was a mere twenty feet behind her—I was going to make it, no problem. She put her foot on the pedal, looked over her shoulder, raised her tiny spandexed ass and shot off over the curb onto the street and blended in with the car traffic.

Damn it. Damn it. Damn it. My target...there she was at the red light. I could do this. I stiff-armed a guy with brochures, hopped over a hydrant and dashed around a kid with a backpack on wheels...it's a freaking backpack, dude, pick it up and put it on your *back*. Run, run, run, breathe, run. Don't. Let. Heart. Explode.

I almost had her. I ran across the traffic as she turned left at her now-green light. I could catch her. I lost sight of her as she rounded the corner. I raced out past the same corner, onto the river walk, barely twenty seconds after her, yet she was nowhere, and I was dying. I slowed to a jog, my head on a swivel looking for the peach top. Nothing.

I panted over to a bench, stretched my hamstrings in defeat and checked my watch. 2:29. I slouched down on the bench until the back of my head rested against the wooden slat and closed my eyes. Damn Swedes. I could have had her...

The honking of horns and small talk of walkers around me changed into the sounds of a different setting. I didn't have to open my eyes to determine the origins of the new noises; a Tilt-A-Whirl wobbled and spun against the backdrop of my closed eyelids. The sun, sharper and warmer than the sun I had just run under, created a glow around the carnival ride. The lilt of music reached my ears at the same time that salty sea air tickled its way into my lungs.

I didn't want to be one of those people who fell asleep on park benches, but I didn't want to open my eyes either. I let my private film play out despite my fear that it was the warm-up for a full-blown dream of an exhausted runner. The Tilt-A-Whirl stopped and happy, dizzy faces hung out over the safety bars. I watched the back of a scrawny carny as she unlocked each safety bar so that the passengers could laugh at their crooked paths away from the ride. She needed a good meal. Her blue work shirt hung limp around her shoulders and hips. She moved in a way that was sultry yet quick and efficient. The jeans on her thin legs were faded and soft, and they ended above her tan ankles, making me think she had a good sense of style but was likely out of cash.

In the back pocket of her jeans, she'd tucked a thin paperback. I could see the top line of the title. "The Handmaid's," it read. Could she be reading *The Handmaid's Tale* by Margaret Atwood? Was she a student who was moonlighting as a Tilt-A-Whirl operator? Or was she a Tilt-A-Whirl operator moonlighting as a philosopher?

She turned to free the last car's passengers, and my stomach plummeted. I spied my own profile on the woman's head. It was *me* again. *I* was opening Tilt-A-Whirl safety bars for carnival goers. *I* was malnourished and sexy. I had never thought of myself as either, but I couldn't deny the evidence of my own eyes. That woman was *me*.

CHAPTER SIX

Without Further Ado

"I daresay none of you know exactly what you are missing out on by being straight," I said. I cleared my throat.

Mascara-coated lashes lowered; manicured hands patted sterile white linens to tense mouths; tickles in throats were damned and swallowed twice, three times in hopes of not escaping. Breaths were held. I looked down at my black velvet jacket and gray velvet pants and wondered if I wasn't underdressed. Nothing looked secondhand, like it was, but I should have maybe thrown on a choker or, God forbid, pearls or something. I looked back at the affluent audience. No, I wasn't underdressed; they were simply overdressed. I continued my speech.

"Not having to think twice about putting a picture of your sweetheart on your desk at work. Not having to think twice about bringing her along to a work social function and subjecting her to narrow-mindedness. Not having to wonder if you didn't get the promotion because the boss is worried you will succumb to the wiles of his secretary and leave him in the dirt. Not having to get pregnant at age fifteen just to prove you are 'normal.'" I pictured Whitney's pain from Thirsty Thursday. I took a deep breath, and I concentrated on not crying for my friend. I refocused on the audience.

"Not having to defend your attractions. Not having to tell people you are not attracted to all women, just this one. Not having to hold your breath until neighbors in your own state decide if you are worthy of basic human rights or if the right to marriage should be constitutionally stolen from you. Not having to stand in front of a terribly large audience like a bacterium under a microscope and explain your love life in twenty minutes or less. That is what you are all missing out on—if you are heterosexual, that is. And that is not to say I am presuming you are hetero."

Did I take it too far with the bacterium bit? I did not chance a look at my mother, sitting in the exact middle of her hive like a queen surrounded by her adoring drones. I listened to the appreciative, relieved laughter that rose and faded gently enough to open the floor for me to continue.

"You are also missing out on having to dash your parents' dreams for you with one sentence—'Mom, I'm gay.' You don't get to experience the joys of avoiding small towns because in a moment of high self-esteem and invulnerability you slapped a rainbow on the back window of your car. You don't get to wonder if you are the token at this party or on this team or in this department. You don't get to think twice and then decide against complimenting a colleague of the same sex."

A long-haired, copper-colored head in the second row of dinner tables caught my eye. The woman was wearing a brilliant blue strapless evening gown that defied gravity as it clung to her thin frame. She was looking down at something below the tabletop. I went on speaking, but I concentrated on the top of the woman's head. I willed her to look up at me.

"You don't have the luxury of inadvertently ending a conversation with the admission that, no, you are not married, no, not really, not in the eyes of the court anyway, but that you and your life partner have been together for twenty-six years and have raised three healthy, well-adjusted kids."

I was speaking too quickly. The copper-haired head looked up at me, and it wasn't the face I feared I might see—me looking back at myself. The vision, if I could call it that, that I had had after my fartlek run was not repeating itself. All that this woman had in common with me was hair color. Her face was wide and freckled with a cute snub-nose and dimpled chin. She didn't have angular cheekbones or a narrow nose like mine. And I had no dimple. She was not me. I slowed down my pace and continued pacifying my mother.

Asha was home alone tonight. I *should* speed through this thing. I should start saying no to my mother. I should...I dropped a note card. The podium's lip caught it for me, so I picked it up and continued. I *should* pay attention. Here was an audience willing to hear about LGBT and Q issues. They were here by choice, they had paid over two hundred dollars a plate tonight and regardless of how I felt about my mother, they deserved a decent speaker even if their two hundred dollars were a tax-deductible charitable contribution to the PDOC foundation. And what about my gay comrades? They deserved to have me do my best in representing them tonight as well.

I concluded my speech by saying, "On the other hand, unless you are differently oriented, you don't have the joy of people around you embracing you for who you are, you don't have the incredible feeling that comes from people accepting you despite the fact that there are others out there telling them not to accept you because you love the wrong gender. So thank you, all of you, for being loving, supportive people."

Afterward, I sat at the table my mother had assigned me to. Two hetero couples greeted me with falsely white, perfect smiles. All four were so coiffed, polished and enhanced that I wondered if my mother placed me at their table to punish me. There were plenty of normal, approachable people here tonight. Sitting with anyone else would have been easier. Instead of worrying about the now-whispering couples, I thought back over my speech. I wished Asha had been there to hear that the few days of having to placate and tolerate my nervous, whiny fears were worth it. I didn't use any of her story but rather stuck to the general issues. My speech had been well received as a whole, and I felt that I had represented the LGBT and Q population with a strong, reasonable voice.

I nursed a red wine someone had placed in my hand and thought that maybe I should have told a few personal stories. Weren't personal stories the elements that made topics understandable for people? Maybe I could volunteer to give another PDOC speech sometime. The stilted tittering and simpering of my table's other inhabitants pulled me from my thoughts for a moment. No. The thought of making my mother shine even that much more brightly because she had raised a well-spoken lesbian was no lure for me. I pictured her with the back of her ivory hand to her alabaster, crease-free forehead murmuring, "Oh, it's just so difficult to protect a differently oriented child these days." Okay then, no more speeches.

I watched people start to fill the dance floor as the band opened with a song I didn't recognize. Both couples at my table excused themselves and made their way to the throng of well-suited and -booted waltzers. I looked for my father and spotted him listening in at the edge of a large conversation that was being led by none other than my mother. Her diamond earrings glinted coldly against her neck, and I felt a pang of sadness for my father. He had to put up with so much princess bullshit with that woman. I watched his face show the practiced anticipation for the end of her story, no doubt one he had heard before at other parties, and I thought that deep down he was a good man.

This wouldn't be his scene if not for my mother's need to shine. No, he'd be much more comfortable practicing medicine in a small town, fishing on the weekends, taking his car through the whatever local, kid-run carwash fundraiser going on in the grocery store parking lot. That was more his speed. But that was only a guess since I'd only ever known him with *her*.

My thoughts turned to Whitney again. A heavy guilt washed over me as I remembered how I used to make believe that I was adopted, that my parents were not really my parents, especially my mother, and that my real mother wanted to have me back. In some of my earlier fantasies she'd arrive on a beautiful green bike built for two, and she'd pedal me away from the school playground. We'd bike over to my house and pick up Guadalupe, my nanny. We'd have Lupe perch on the front handlebars, and we'd wheel off into our new life—the life I was meant to live. In other fantasies, as I got older, my real mom would drive up to the high school steps in a mysterious black Saab—with a ski rack on top—and she'd honk until I broke out of my last class and ran down the steps to be enveloped in her car and waiting arms. Eventually I gave up the fantasies and admitted that these were my parents and I was stuck in this family regardless of how alien it felt at times. I was embarrassingly old, though, before I gave up the hope.

I looked at my wineglass, the level barely dented by my two or three meager sips. I needed to walk around, get some fresh thoughts and maybe a happier perspective. I abandoned my wine and headed for the restroom.

Was Whitney's daughter looking for Whitney, her biological mother, because she was in a loveless situation with her adoptive family? Or was she merely curious? Would Whit be receptive to talk about this? Alone with me, or maybe with Asha and me? I decided to call her tomorrow to see how she was doing. Maybe she *needed* to talk it all through.

I passed a few small groups of chatting, polished, perfumed people in the elegant reception chamber that I had to go through to reach the hallway with the restrooms. The hallway was lavish with ornate floor-to-ceiling mirrors and paintings of hillsides dotted with golden rural homes. The spindly tables beside the mirrors were artsy with their worn white paint giving way to soft wood. It was King Louis XVI meets the French countryside and everything had a calculated touch of understated class.

I glanced at my reflection in one of the huge mirrors and was happy to notice that I didn't look as tired as I felt. My hair, loose yet somewhat tamed, was as shiny as a new penny and about the same color as one too. Maybe a little darker. I had good color in my cheekbones and my eyes were bright enough. Seeing myself made me feel less weary. And thinking that it would be a long time before I'd have to do another favor for my mother was like a shot of caffeine. I smiled at myself and entered the women's restroom.

Inside the door three women were talking and peering down at a tiny handbag being held out by the shortest of the three women. They were inspecting it—checking to see if it were authentic, I guessed. Soft music floated around them like a mink mantle. More mirrors, two small brown sofas and a pink velvet chaise lounge edged the big room. Where the hell was the actual restroom? I spotted a door beside the chaise lounge.

"I only paid two-twenty-nine for it!" the petite woman gushed. Diamonds glinted on most of her fingers.

"A steal," another woman said. "I'm envious."

It was a steal, I knew, if it was real, and it probably was. I pushed open the door to the toilet and sink area. This area was no less plush. As the door shut to the outer room, the women's voices were muted, but the soft music still flowed about me. Some women—my mother, for example—thought nothing of dropping thousands on a handbag. How ridiculous it was, when all that money could have gone to something meaningful. I mused over how everyone was here tonight to raise money for the PDOC charity, yet really it was more of a catwalk showcasing who was who and who was wearing or carrying what. That two-twenty-nine could have gone to charity. Where did the PDOC money go anyway?

I chose the first stall, ornate with thickly opaque frosted glass. I didn't really even have to go. I just wanted to not be surrounded by people. But as long as I was there, I took care of what little business I could, stood up, marveled over the quietest automatic flush I'd ever witnessed and headed out to wash my hands. I let the warm water run over my hands as I leaned against the marble countertop. I closed my eyes and listened as...

The classical music gave way to the jangling, jaunty notes of a pipe organ or some electric piano type of instrument. I smiled to hear the joyous cries of children and the barking voice of a man trying to attract a crowd. When I opened my eyes, bright, colorful lights were bouncing off a luminescent indigo sky that lost itself in the ocean. I looked over my shoulder and saw the sun's final vestiges creating a golden outline of buildings as it sank behind the coastal town. Turning back to face the endless expanse of water, I realized it was just after sunset. Legs dangled above me, wheeling and spinning from chairs suspended on a circular swing ride.

On the ground there were sweethearts walking arm and arm, smiling at each other over paper buckets of cookies and popcorn; there were people with small children hoisted onto their shoulders and other children looking backward while walking forward, being dragged by the hand to the next adventure; and there were teenagers with bright eyes and carefully haphazard hairstyles walking slowly enough to be noticed but not so slowly that anyone would be able to fill their eyes with them. And off to the left in front of me, at the farthest reach of the carnival, her elbows on the wooden railing that separated the carnival from the ocean, stood...me. I was there.

Since the sun had set moments ago, all that was left of its light were thousands of glittery orange stains glowing at the crest of each small wave. They disappeared where the water met the bottom of the dark blue sky. The soft yellow hooded sweatshirt I was wearing must not have been warm enough because I appeared to be shivering. I held my arms wrapped about my torso. I watched, spellbound at seeing how thin and forlorn I had become, as I released myself from my own hug, held the railing before me and leaned back, looking up at the night sky. I found myself following my gaze to the sky, and I was surprised I could see no stars.

I watched, then, as I stood up straight, wiped my face and turned away from the water. My heart tightened when I saw how drawn I looked. I had been crying. I wiped my face one last time, pushed my hands into the front pocket of my hoodie and walked toward me. I turned to watch myself pass and saw that I was heading to the Tilt-A-Whirl. I saw myself have a few quiet words with the woman who had been operating the ride. She patted me on my shoulder and turned the controls over to me.

What was going on? The jangly carnival music lost it edges, and I could detect strains of wind and string instruments blending in and then standing out and...

Now I only heard classical music. The sensation of warm water cascading over my hands prompted me to open my eyes. I was staring at myself, the self I knew and recognized, in the mirror. Another woman had come into the restroom and was just closing herself in behind a stall door. I shook my head to try to clear it, dried my hands and left.

Back in the main hall, a passing waiter handed me a glass of red wine.

"No, thank you—" I protested, but to no avail. He nodded at me and was half a table away before I even lifted the glass back in his direction. I sipped it, since it looked like I was stuck with it.

I sat down in an empty chair. I felt knackered. Why was I seeing myself like this? What was I supposed to do about it? I closed my eyes and rubbed my forehead between my eyebrows and tried not to think about it, but I found that the visions were all I *could* think of. I wanted to go home.

I stood and turned to make my way to the parking lot. My job here was done, and I knew Asha waited. Realizing that I was still clutching the stem of a full glass of merlot, I sought out a sparsely populated table on which to leave it. Instead of making an unnoticed exit, I collided hard with the front of an elderly man who must have been turning at exactly the same time I was. We sputtered "Oh!" at the same time, and I grabbed my now empty wineglass with both hands as the man grabbed my arms to steady me.

As soon as the man determined I was steady enough to let go of, he ran his hands through the shock of salt-and-pepper hair that had sprung over his forehead, trying to tame his unruly locks. He managed to bring order to almost every strand save one that defied gravity.

"Dr. Windler, my deepest apologies." It was Dr. Pinehurst! Curiosity about why he might be at the PDOC event quickly gave way to concern about the merlot stain that marred almost the entire visible surface of his white shirt and one lapel of his dark gray suit jacket.

"Ohhh, Dr. Pinehurst…Art! I am so sorry!" I set the glass down on the nearest table and looked around for a napkin or something to blot the wine from his clothing. There was nothing within reach but white linen, and none of the napkins appeared to be without owners. Most people nearby were glancing at us while trying to appear as if they were minding their own business, but one woman pressed her linen napkin into Arthur's hand. He dabbed half-heartedly at the stain.

"It's nothing," he said. "A good excuse to buy a new shirt." He smiled at me and leaned closer. "A good excuse to leave a little early too," he whispered, still smiling. He straightened up and stopped tending to the stain.

"I'm sorry," I said again. His hair tried to go all Einstein, but he swatted it back into place.

"Your speech was good," he said. "It made us all think, made us notice the things we have the luxury of taking for granted."

"Thank you. It wasn't my best lecture ever, but…"

"It was good," Arthur said. He looked around the hall.

"Art, have you belonged to PDOC long?" I asked. Did he have kids? Gay kids? My question seemed to catch him off guard. He looked down at the bright red splash on his shirt, toyed with his bow tie, which had been spared, and cleared his throat.

"No, not long," he started, then… "Yes, well, in a way." He looked about the hall again.

"Oh," I said, not knowing what else to say. I noticed my father was approaching us.

"Well, Cassie, it was nice running into you here." He smiled with his mouth, but his brown eyes couldn't conceal his uneasiness. "However, I have to be going now. Good job on your speech and have a good evening."

He dipped his head at me in a way that made me think of old-fashioned gentlemen in silent movies. Before my father reached us, Art had disappeared into the throngs of well-dressed mixers and minglers.

"Cassie? Was that Arthur Pinehurst?" My father's voice was pinched in a way I had never heard it before.

"Yes, he had to go, probably because I just managed to dump an entire glass of wine on him," I said. I expected my father to comment on that or to at least chuckle and say these things happen, but he didn't.

"What did he want with you?" he asked instead.

"Well, we banged into each other," I explained, "I don't think he wanted anything with me before that…but we do know each other from school."

"You do? He's back at the U? Why?" My father sounded so unusually sharp that my heartbeat sped up, and I sensed a bit of panic in myself for him.

"Um, he's teaching a few classes?" I said, watching his reaction. What was wrong? My father looked pale. I saw him glance around the room. Was he looking for his charity celeb wife, or was he seeking Dr. Pinehurst?

"I have to go," my father said. For the second time that night I was left standing alone in the middle of the room. Before he left, however, I noticed a definite sheen of perspiration on his forehead. It was not hot in here. No reception hall would dare be anything other than perfectly climate-controlled during one of my mother's events. So what was up? Was he ill? I didn't get the impression that he was. I only got the impression he was very, very nervous. In all my years, I had never seen my father sweat. Not once.

CHAPTER SEVEN

Not Apple Pie Perfect

"I'm afraid I'll hear her voice and lose my mind," Whitney said, her voice barely above a whisper. "I'm afraid I'll go crazy regretting my decision until I just lose all—"

"No, Whit," I tried to soothe her worries, "you won't lose your mind. You might regret things, that's true, but you won't lose your mind."

"Ugh, I feel like I'm losing it already. All I do is think about her emails. Should I reply, should I not reply? I don't know what to do." She ran her hands over her hair, which was tied back in a tight ponytail. Even though she had had it straightened not too long ago, tiny tendrils had sprung out around her face, curling despite her attempts to slick and pull them into submission. The little curls made her look so much like a child. There was pain and indecision in her eyes, and I wished I knew what to say to ease her confusion regarding her biological daughter.

What could one say, though, to a mother who had given up her daughter? That she had done the right thing? Could anyone ever be certain of that? Was there even a good, scientifically reliable way to measure whether adoption had been the right choice for anyone? If I had ever been presented with the choice to give up a baby and had taken that option, what would I have wanted to hear in this scenario?

"Whit, I have to believe, and so do you, that you did the right thing."

"How do you know?" she asked quietly. Then more vehemently, "How do you *know*? How am I supposed to know?"

"You could answer her email and see what she has to say…"

"Yeah," Whitney said. The waiter came at that point and asked if we were interested in dessert. It was November second and my Halloween sugar buzz had worn off, so I craved something sweet. But when I looked to Whitney for her response, she shook her head.

"Thanks, no," I told the waiter. He nodded and turned away. My heart barely had time to mourn the lack of dessert when Whitney called out to him.

"Wait…excuse me, sir?" she called.

"You changed your mind?" he asked, returning with a jovial smile on his face. He stood with pen poised over his small notepad.

"Yes," Whitney said. "But I have a favor to ask of you."

He waggled his eyebrows suggestively, grinning the way only a cute kid who knows he is a cute kid can grin, and said, "Anything you want," in a deeper voice.

"Uhm, yeah, no," Whitney laughed, "not that kind of favor, but thanks. I was hoping you could surprise me with my dessert." What the hell? Who would leave dessert, such an important part of the meal, up to some guy's whim?

"You don't even want to see the menu?" the waiter asked in his normal voice.

"Nope. Can you just surprise me?"

"I can," he replied. "No one has ever asked me to do that before; I like it. I'm going to bring you my favorite." He looked so pleased with himself and the prospect of surprising someone that I asked him to surprise me too, but only with his second favorite. What the heck—you only live once, as far as we know.

And really, any dessert was good dessert. I could see his wheels spinning as he turned away from our table.

"Daring," I said.

"Mmm, we'll see," Whitney replied.

"You know, Whit, I don't know what to say to you, exactly, because I am not sure what it would be like to be in your shoes right now, but…I don't think you can go wrong with emailing her back."

"We'll see. You know, I worry that I will meet her and decide that I gave up the best thing that could ever have happened to me."

"Yeah," I said, "but if you don't email her back, you'll be giving it up twice."

"Wow. That is exactly what Cory said," Whitney mused.

"That Cory is one smart woman," I joked.

"She's been incredible. Not just with this, but with everything. She is so good to me."

I thought of Asha and said, "We're lucky." Whitney smiled at me, and her smile reached deep, deep into my eyes. We *were* lucky.

"I've decided," Whitney began sheepishly, "that if Mr. Hunka Hunka Burnin' Love here brings me apple pie, I will not email her back. But if it's anything else, anything other than apple pie, I will email her tonight when I get home."

"Again, I say 'daring,'" I said, "and I like your plan." I secretly hoped apple pie wasn't even on the menu. I felt like Whitney would never forgive herself if she didn't at least answer her daughter's email.

We didn't talk again until the waiter came with a crème brulée in one hand and some sort of fudgey, cakey, gooey goodness in the other. This he set down in front of Whitney. A sob escaped her throat, and she put both hands up to her face and began to cry into them. The waiter's eyes opened wide, and his pride in his surprise was wiped from his face in one instant. He picked up the plate he had just set in front of her.

"It's okay, it's okay, I can get something else for you. It's okay!" he said.

"No, no," I told him, "it's perfect—it's not apple pie, so it's perfect."

"You sure?" he asked, his eyebrows knitting together, and I noticed how very cute he really was. He'd make a nice son for someone, I thought.

"I'm sure. You just helped her make a decision, and…" I didn't know what else to say, so I let the sentence trail off. Whitney sobbed.

"She's scared?" he guessed. "And happy?"

"Exactly, and you are perfect," I told him, looking him straight in the eye so he knew I meant it. "Thank you." I smiled at him, and he smiled back.

"Don't be scared," he said to Whitney. He put an awkward hand on her heaving shoulder. "You can do it, whatever it is." He looked at me, and I saw we were both in jeopardy of joining in Whitney's tears, so I took the crème brulée he was still holding out in the air above our table.

"Thank you," I said again because that was all I could muster.

"Thank you," he said. He gave Whitney's shoulder one last pat, and he turned to attend to others. He'd be getting a big tip tonight, I decided.

CHAPTER EIGHT

Preparing the Past

"You can't change the future, only the past."

"I don't know what you mean, Lupe," I said.

I didn't know if her words were the painkillers talking or the wisdom that comes from being deathly ill, but I couldn't fathom how a person could change the past. My aging nanny's hair fell like a steel cascade and pooled about her shoulders in the hospital gown. Nothing changed about the intensity of the love in her gaze on me, but the intensity of her as a whole was diminished. She was gaunt and her warm brown skin had paled into a café au lait. She had called from the hospital to let me know she was there, but she asked me not to tell my parents just yet.

"The future is set, to the final degree, no?" She looked at me with her smile gentle and her eyes sad. "We know how things will end for each of us…some variation of this." With effort, she waved her hand to indicate her surroundings. She pressed her lips together and smiled again, but it still didn't reach her eyes.

"That's true," I said.

Was she ready to die? She was only sixty-one. She had dealt with a terminal cancer for the past eight months and only now needed hospitalization. She had no family in the US other than my parents and me, yet she had several solid friendships with other immigrant women her age. These friends had helped Guadalupe as much as they could before they finally, hesitantly suggested it was time to go to the hospital for more than just blood work and medication.

"But how can you change the past?" I asked.

I was used to not understanding Lupe's perspective at first hearing, but almost always, after chewing on her words, letting them play, testing them with different sets of taste buds, running my tongue over them like a troublesome chipped tooth, I'd find the sharp, bright edge and appreciate the new awareness her words brought. She was the wisest person I had ever met, as well as the most caring. When I was in middle school, I taught Guadalupe to read and write in English, and she taught me how it felt to trust a person implicitly. She never abandoned me, emotionally or physically. Every day after I left the yellow school bus behind, she greeted me with a warm hug, a gleaming smile and big dictionary words bubbling out in her heavy Spanish accent. I wasn't ready for her to be gone, even if she was ready to go.

"Our pasts are changed by us all the time, Bodoquito, in the way we remember them. The way we talk to ourselves about our pasts…or tell others…this creates new pasts always, all the time, no?"

"Well, no."

The woman who was closer to me than my own mother had ever been was dying, and I was going to argue with her. I was. Because it made me feel normal and like I *might* be able to control the future. I wondered if I should ask Lupe about the visions I was having.

"Yes, it does create new pasts," she retorted. Good, this was normal. She had the strength to teach me, her obstinate student.

"Lupe, we can't change the past. We can't. It's already… done. It's set in stone."

"Whose stone?" The ferocity of her question brought her to a coughing fit. I offered her water from the cup on the sterile little bedside table, but she shook her head at it.

"What do you mean, 'Whose stone?' My stone, your stone, I don't know...*the* stone...the past is the past...irrefutable." Why did I want to add, "Right?" The past was what it was, unchangeable. The future, however...I felt it wouldn't be fair to bring my stress to Lupe by telling her, asking her, about my visions. I'd do that when she was healthier. I had the feeling she'd be able to shed some light on these troubling images of myself, but just not right now.

"*Mi mitad de la Bodoquito*, what is your earliest memory?" She was serious when she called me by my full name, My Half Bundle.

"My what?" What did my earliest memory have to do with anything?

"Your earliest memory, tell me, what is it?"

Surrounded by her failing body, the fire of making me understand burned in her eyes. Lupe's eyes were my earliest memory, if I thought back far enough. Her eyes like warm charcoal and her voice. Her voice fanning the flame of the heat of her eyes, singing to me until I understood that I was safe. That was my earliest memory.

"Lupe, my earliest memory is of you singing to me."

Lupe was silent. She pursed her lips, closed her eyes, and I took her hand in mine.

"Are you in pain? Are you okay, Lu?"

I heard the fear in my voice, and I was caught off guard. Of course she was okay. She was Guadalupe. Guadalupe was okay so that the rest of the world could be okay. She was fine.

"I'm okay, child. I am touched, that is all."

She coughed like an infant asleep. She kept her eyes closed. I didn't feel it fair to pester her about changing the past, so I sat and held her hand. A nurse came in, all starch and cardboard cutout in her uniform, and asked Lupe how she was feeling as she recorded the numbers on the two machines that Lupe was connected to. Lupe told her she was fine, of course. Even if she weren't fine, this would be her answer. I could surmise nothing from the nurse's bland face as she made notes in Lupe's file. Lupe's hand in mine gave a feeble squeeze. She had been looking at me as I searched the nurse's face.

"I'm fine, Bodoquito, I really am fine," she told me.

"Lupe, can you come home with me? Let me take care of you?"

"No, thank you," she replied. "I need to stay here for now… too many medicines, machines, too many things to go home with you." The nurse nodded and left the room.

"What about radiation then? Or chemo, what about chemo?"

"No, I'm okay just like this. The doctors told me about radiations and chemo and I do not like the sound of that. I'll be just fine right here."

Lupe coughed roughly, her chest echoing. I looked at Lupe's hand in mine. It was small and mottled. Tears pooled at the back of my throat.

"Don't be sad, Bodoquito, don't be sad," Lupe whispered. She stifled another cough. Her throat made dry rasps and her chest heaved, but she didn't let the cough surface. She sounded hollow.

"I have something important to tell you, child," she continued. "I have to tell you how your past was changed. Something you need to know."

She cleared her throat to say more, but the coughing that she had suppressed came roaring out. She hacked and sputtered from deep within her fragile chest. My heart began breaking silently inside of my own fragile chest, and I didn't stop the tears this time. Through the blur, I spied the cup of water again, and this time I brought it to her lips without waiting for her assent. Between rasps, she sipped and choked down water. The nurse appeared, like an action figure brought to life by Lupe's wracks.

"Okay, Ms. Lagunas, okay," she took the water from my hand and set it on the table, stepping between Lupe and me. She pressed Lupe, placing one hand on her chest and the other behind her back, bent Lupe forward, and began pelting her back with dangerous, firm smacks. Lupe's cough died down and then out. "It's all right, Ms. Lagunas, you just keep taking breaths; you're okay." I continued crying silently as Lupe worked on breathing.

CHAPTER NINE

The Proposal

Asha's eyes filled with tears as I told her about my visit to Guadalupe that afternoon and what the nurse had told me as I was leaving. I took off my glasses, and Asha took them from me and set them on the coffee table. She pulled me down into her lap and held me until my own renewed tears were depleted. My hair was sticking to the side of my face, and this she smoothed back so that she could kiss my temple as she cradled me in her arms. She smelled of sawdust and Issey Miyake, and I was comforted by her familiar scent.

"I'm going to mess up my mascara," I said, sitting up in her lap, pulling myself away from her embrace. She held tight to my arms and pulled me back toward her. She kissed me between my eyes, her lips warm and dry on my forehead.

"Just relax, our reservation will be held. Tell me what you think is going to happen with Lupe."

I inhaled until my lungs wouldn't take any more air. I held my breath until they began to ache.

"Cass, baby, breathe," Asha said, her lips against my head. "What do you think is happening with Lupe?"

"She's dying." All my breath tumbled the words out and sobs followed the words.

I burrowed into Asha's shoulder and let all my fears line up in front of me like a firing squad. Guadalupe was dying. Guadalupe loved me more than my own mother did. I loved Guadalupe more than I loved my mother. She was in pain. She wouldn't be here for me; I wouldn't get to be there for her. We wouldn't get to see each other get really old. Asha petted the back of my head as I cried. She made little humming noises that I could hear each time I inhaled. My heart swelled with love for her even as it shrank with fear over losing Guadalupe. After a while, I stopped crying.

"Cassie?"

"Mm hmm."

"Do you want to stay in tonight?"

"Yeah. Do you mind?" I asked.

Asha had planned a dinner out at a restaurant for our anniversary. I didn't want her to be disappointed, but I couldn't imagine sitting with a bunch of strangers, trying to eat.

"No, I don't. I'll cook here, okay?"

I nodded.

"Why don't you make a list of the things you need to talk to Guadalupe about before…?" Asha's voice died out.

That sounded like a good idea. Like something I could control. So as Asha stirred Thai noodles at the stove, I sat at the counter and began creating a list. This was a balm for my aching heart, and I was surprised that taking steps toward a life without Lupe calmed me. How could there be a life without her?

So far I had written that I needed to get updated addresses of her extended family in Mexico. She had two brothers, and they'd want to know she was sick. Next I wrote that I wanted to hear about how she came to be employed by my parents. We'd never spoken about that. I knew she was undocumented, which was the reason her brothers had come here to visit her rather than her going to Mexico to visit them, but we had never spoken of how she found my parents or how they'd found her. They still gave her a salary despite the fact that she rarely did anything for them anymore, but beyond that, I didn't know what kind of arrangements had been made for her health care or…anything. She was in the hospital, and that bill wasn't going to pay itself.

I also wrote down that I wanted to ask her about the visions I was having. She might know why and how I was seeing myself a few years down the road. If she didn't know for certain, I had a feeling she'd be able to at least tell me how to deal with the visions. Maybe she'd even know how to stop them. Just in case my list became public, I disguised this item as "question about the boardwalk." That should be vague and non-incriminating enough for Asha's eyes—or anyone else's, for that matter.

Then I wrote that I wanted Lupe to tell me about what she meant about changing the past and specifically what she meant when she'd said my past had been changed. I let my glasses slide down my nose a bit and rubbed my forehead between my eyebrows.

"What have you got so far?" Asha wanted to know. She blew on a noodle and held it out for me to test. I grabbed it with my mouth, feeling like a baby bird. The end of the noodle whapped against my chin. I felt its sticky sauce leave a trail, so I grabbed the dishtowel and cleaned up. Asha was smiling at me when I finished.

"They're ready," I laughed, "and they're really tasty."

I was feeling a little bit better. I hopped off my chair and tested, more neatly this time, a few more noodles for good measure. I read Asha my list for Lupe, everything except for the question about the boardwalk visions. I didn't want Asha thinking I was crazy, even though I was beginning to think I might very well be. Asha was intrigued by the idea of changing the past.

"I'd like to know more about that as soon as you know," she said. "But first," she took my Lupe list from my hands and laid it on the countertop, "first I need to ask you about changing our future."

She grabbed me by the hips, lifted me to the countertop and set me beside my list. The fridge was opened and closed, emptier by one bottle of Veuve Clicquot. Wasabi appeared beside me on the countertop to whisker the bottle and rub her head on my hip.

"No, Wasi, get off the counter," I said.

I scooted her to the floor where she slalomed between Asha's ankles. Asha ignored her as best she could without stepping on her as she poured two glasses of champagne. Mmm-hmmm... what was up here? A ridiculous number of bubbles celebrated in my glass as Asha handed it to me. Asha looked very serious. She got down on one knee and Wasabi planted her furry butt on the kitchen floor beside her. Asha had to crane her neck to keep eye contact with me all the way up on the counter. I smiled and my heart filled with the same ridiculous number of champagne bubbles. I knew where she was going with this. Asha's straight face finally broke into a grin. Asha stood up and pressed her hips to my knees, a much better angle for eye contact.

"Cassie," Asha began.

She took a visibly deep breath and plunged her hand into her pants pocket. She withdrew a ring box, took one of my hands in hers and placed the box in my open palm.

"Cass, you are my favorite person in the whole wide world. You light up my heart, my home and my...bed." She laughed at the end of her sentence, and I did too.

She nuzzled my forehead with hers, holding my hand closed around the ring box. I stopped laughing, but I couldn't stop smiling.

"I know," she took another deep breath before continuing, "I know that this is terribly cliché and that maybe it doesn't mean anything to anyone outside of us, but I want to spend the rest of my life with you, and I love you more than I ever knew a person could love another, and..."

I didn't know when I had stopped breathing, but when Asha took another deep breath, I did too.

"Cassie Windler, will you be my unlawfully wedded wife?"

CHAPTER TEN

Updates and Downswings

"Relationship status…" I said out loud but quietly to myself in my U of M office.

If a person's going to suffer hallucinations, talk to herself and be ecstatic, she might at least keep her voice lowered. I scanned the list of choices for describing my life's details on my Facebook account. "It's complicated," "in a relationship," "married"—no, no and, no.

"'Engaged!'" I said out loud again and more loudly this time.

I was excited. I hit the enter key with gusto and leaned back in my chair, grinning, my hands clasped over my belly like a happy Buddha. I had been surprised by Asha's proposal; we had never really talked much about marriage. Since the marriage that would afford us the legal advantages that heterosexual couples have, such as not having to pay tax on spousal inheritance and not having to fight for hospital visitation rights, was not an option for us, we hadn't discussed the topic at any great length. It was as if we were holding our breath. Despite the upcoming election and the impressive number of "Vote No" on banning same-sex marriage bumper stickers I'd seen plastered on cars around the Twin Cities, I wasn't convinced legal marriage was anywhere near in our future in Minnesota.

Late into last night, Asha and I had planned our ideal commitment ceremony. We would host a smallish affair at our house. The backyard had lovely old lilacs that bloomed most vibrantly near the end of spring, so we picked Saturday, May 18, which was also the end of my school year at the U. We decided to ask Esme to sing because she had a booming, warm, wonderful voice, and she enjoyed performing. Asha suggested a Caribbean theme, since Esme's songs would undoubtedly be from the islands, but I had to think about that. I wasn't sure we needed a theme since "backyard" was, quite possibly, theme enough.

We hadn't yet decided on the food. I wanted desserts and champagne so that it could be a late evening affair and we wouldn't have to worry about a big meal, but Asha was leaning toward the full meal deal. I didn't know where people would all sit to eat, but Asha wasn't concerned about that. She said they'd eat wherever they landed. Some would eat outside at a few small tables we could get, and some would eat inside at the breakfast bar or the dining room. She said people would be happy to stand around or sit on the couch to eat as well. Thinking about it now, I had to admit that her plan would have the advantages of not having to worry about timing or big toasts or glasses being clinked for kisses.

Right before we had fallen asleep, Asha had asked, "Cass, do you think you'll wear a white dress?"

I almost gagged for fun, but then I realized, from the sound of her voice in the dark, that she was being sincere.

"Do you want me to?"

"Yes…" she replied, "if you are comfortable, you know."

"Okay," I said, picturing myself. "I'll wear a white dress."

"Cool," she said and leaned over me to kiss me one last time goodnight. "Cool," she had whispered. She had been smiling. I could hear it in the dark.

A white dress is what I probably would have worn even without Asha's request, despite the fact that I had always found it delicious to make gentle fun of hetero couples and some of their traditions. I thought I mostly did that out of jealousy and to convince myself that I didn't really want everything that they have that is so sacred, protected and exclusive anyway.

A bing from my computer interrupted my thoughts. It was a message from Michael.

"Congratulations, Wind!"

It was nice to see his message, and I was about to respond when there was a series of bings letting me know more friends had just read and felt compelled to comment on my new status.

"So, so, so happy for you, Cassie," wrote Esme.

"Congratulations, you two!" Desiree, one of Asha's colleagues wrote.

"It is about damn time!" Jenn wrote.

Didn't anyone work these days? It was mid-afternoon. How could all these people be on Facebook now?

"Seriously? When is the big day?" asked Lucas Wintersmith, a friend from my childhood school days.

"Why didn't you tell me?" Asha wrote. What?

"Brilliant! Congratulations! When is the ceremony? I'll try to be in town for you two!" wrote Linda Crespo, an old U of M colleague who had gone to teach on the West Coast.

"Just kidding, my sweet fiancée!" Asha wrote.

Ah, I got it. I clicked "Like" under Asha's comment and checked the time. 2:28. No, make that 2:29, I thought, as the number at the top of my computer screen changed. I leaned back in my chair again and spun in lazy half-circles, thinking of my wife-to-be. I closed my eyes and enjoyed the ache in my cheeks from smiling so hard. Another bing let me know someone else had commented on my newly updated status. I'd look in a minute. And…

Another bing. Okay. I opened my eyes just in time to see myself taking a little pastry out of the microwave in a tiny kitchen. I tossed it back and forth between my hands—it must have been hot.

"Going to work, Ax," I yelled. There was an unfamiliar, but sweet twang to the words I was calling out. "I'll see you later!"

"Grab some dinner on your way back," a thick, tired-sounding voice called back to me. "There's nothing in the fridge again. Get some beer too."

I placed the pastry on the counter as I used my hands to tuck a copy of Oscar Wilde's *The Picture of Dorian Gray* into my back pocket. A rugged, unshaven man rounded the corner into the kitchen. His eyes were soft and sleepy. Bare-chested but boxer-clad, he held his arms out to me. He was sexy in a bad boy sort of way, like a movie character for whom you want to witness a life-changing, clean-up-your-act-but-still-stay-sexy event. I felt as if I had seen his face somewhere before...perhaps in a dream.

"C'mere," he said.

I could see myself relaxing. I gave my paperback one more shove to make it stay in my pocket, and then I went to him. I snuggled my shoulders under his arms. He held me, still and silent, for a moment, and then he raised one hand to pet my hair. Three times he ran his hand from the top of my head to the ends of my hair at the middle of my back. His gentleness was what one would expect from a man with those soft eyes, now closed.

"Thank you, Axel," I murmured into his chest. I watched myself as I breathed deeply and I knew I was trying to gather the best of him so I could keep that part of him with me all day.

"Have fun today," he said.

He kissed the top of my head. Then he pressed his fingers under my chin and tipped my face up for a long, soft kiss.

"You too," I said.

I watched myself pull out of his arms, press one thin fingertip to his lips and with my own lips blow him a kiss. I smiled at him. He smiled in return and sauntered out of the kitchen. I picked up the still hot pastry and tossed it back and forth again, waiting for it to cool.

"Don't forget the beer," Axel reminded from the other room.

"I'll take care of it, see you later," I called before opening a door that had been painted white on the kitchen side but was dark brown on the other side.

I watched and followed as I lightly ran down wooden steps carpeted with a dingy brown utility runner. I entered a large room, a bar and restaurant that I had seen before. I recognized the big blonde behind the bar. She threw a towel over her shoulder and stacked a few glasses on a high shelf behind the counter before turning to wave me off.

"Hey, Peej," it sounded like she said.

"Hey," I heard myself say. I watched as I looked around the deserted room. "Why's it so empty?"

"Dunno," the blonde said. "Been quiet all day, you know?"

"Huh. Well, I'm late—I'll see you after my shift. Have a good night. Hope it picks up for ya."

"Yeah, me, too. And thanks, you too." The woman waved again, and I followed myself out into the bright, bright morning sunlight. From the top of the road, I could see the boardwalk in front of me. The sun, newly risen from the ocean, cast millions of sparkling shards in my direction. I squinted and then gave in and closed my eyes against the glare.

When I hesitantly reopened them, I was greeted by Hello Kitty hanging on my office wall. I had just seen my future with a man. I had nothing against men. But to *be* with one? Me? Where was Asha? What was happening? I felt strange. I was beginning to think seriously that I needed to have my head examined—for neurological reasons if nothing else. I took off my glasses and set them on a pile of papers atop my desk. I rested my forehead in my palm, taking care that I didn't inadvertently close my eyes. I wanted to stay right *here*, not open my eyes to the boardwalk or to wherever the other me was headed. What was *wrong* with me?

There were many reasons a person could have sensory misperceptions, I knew, and most of them would not send a person running to a psychiatrist. The least likely of the reasons was that I was having a psychodynamic disturbance where my unconscious perceptions were leaking into my consciousness.

I may have considered this if the visions weren't of me in the future. I could tell from how tired and worn out I appeared in the visions that I was projecting myself to some later date. Is that what I was doing, then? Projecting myself? Were these my fears materializing? No, I didn't think so.

So that left something psychophysiological, where something had messed with my brain's structure, or perhaps psychobiochemical, where something was disrupting my neurotransmitters.

This was giving me a headache. It was much easier to kick these ideas around while researching somebody other than myself. I massaged my forehead with the heel of my palm and abruptly stopped when I realized the cause of the visions could be a brain lesion or tumor. Or maybe some other disease. Didn't Creutzfeldt-Jakob disease sufferers experience visions?

I combed through my memory. No, they experienced color changes and other visual defects. So back to the tumor then. Peduncular hallucinosis, maybe? Seeing full-blown scenes involving animals and characters was symptomatic of peduncular hallucinations. And they were brought on by…what? I groaned and leaned back in my chair. Brain tumors and lesions. Damn this.

I wanted so badly to ask someone about these visions, these "me" sightings, but I was afraid to because I didn't know exactly how to describe them and I didn't want anyone to worry about me losing my marbles. Though that might be what was happening here—which might be better than a brain tumor. I should tell someone, get help retaining the few marbles I had left. Most of all I wanted to tell Asha. It felt so foreign to have an experience that I couldn't share with her. But of all people, she was the very last one I'd want worrying about my sanity. A psych ward would not make a good location for a honeymoon. It'd be memorable, yes, but not good.

CHAPTER ELEVEN

Saints

Michael laced up his running shoes.

"Thanks, Windler, for getting me out of the office. Been a long week."

"Mmm…" I took the ponytail holder out of my mouth and put my hair up. "Thank you for coming with me. Your water bottle," I said and pointed so he wouldn't forget it. I wanted to take advantage of the fact that it hadn't yet snowed, so we were heading out for a Friday run. We left the office, the building and then even the campus behind. I needed to talk to him, to get a reality check, about these vision things, and I had thought for days about where to do this. I had learned from Michael himself where *not* to initiate a serious conversation.

Several years ago he'd joined me and Guadalupe at a Saint Paul Saints game. When he returned from a trip to the concession stand, he was carrying a tray with five hot dogs and three sodas balanced on it—and his grinning face was sporting a glamorous set of long black whiskers and a cat-eyed glittery mask. The grin was his own. The whiskers and mask were the handiwork of the face painter for the independent professional ball team, a woman known as St. Carol. He'd just prayed to her, he told us, adding that he suspected that his wife was having an affair. I was in the process of passing one of the soft drinks to Guadalupe when I realized that his smile was not one of genuine mirth but one that bordered on hysteria. As Guadalupe and I listened to his reasons for thinking Holly was seeing another man, I knew that his marriage was dissolving. His painted face had made the whole conversation surreal.

Another conversation which I had made a mental note not to replicate was the one that had occurred just this past summer after I picked him up to drive him home after his colonoscopy. He had been given a drug that would allow him to not remember the procedure, but apparently the drug also worked akin to a truth serum. As I drove him home, I was made privy to his confessions of myriad minor transgressions—one of them being that he had stolen my stapler and had no intention of returning it to me.

As we began our run, I was happy to not have my face painted nor to have truth serum flowing through my veins. I was also happy to have Michael at my shoulder rather than in front of me, facing me. Side-by-side conversations were always easier than face-to-face ones. I dodged a young woman on a scooter who was backing herself and her vehicle by foot power away from the curb before cranking the scooter on and merging with traffic. Michael grabbed my elbow to steady me. Such a man, thinking I needed assistance.

"Thanks," I panted. Such a woman.

"Yeah," he panted back.

"Hey, I have to ask your opinion," I began.

"Yeah," he repeated.

Where was I supposed to begin? Maybe the colonoscopy truth serum had its benefits. We crossed against the light—it was so much easier when there were two of us—and ran toward St. Paul.

"Have you ever seen yourself in another life, kind of like… well…a vision?" I decided to begin with a question. Maybe this had happened to Michael before, and he'd assure me I was normal—nothing to worry about.

"Like aspiring toward a better you?"

"Uh, no...like seeing yourself right now or maybe in the future, but nothing you aspire to. At all."

We wove around the trees on the boulevard. Ochre leaves clung defiantly to the oaks. They rattled drily in the breeze. All of the other trees were already bare, ready for winter to come.

"I don't think so," Michael answered.

"I mean...have you ever had really clear...lifelike visions of yourself...third person style?" My words came out in bits. I wasn't panting from the run yet, but nerves about putting this topic out there had me a little gaspy.

"How others see you?" He was trying to understand what I was asking. I appreciated this, but at the same time I was growing frustrated that he wasn't getting it. Of course, *I* couldn't comprehend it, so how was he supposed to get it from my lame attempt to ask about it?

"No. Thing is...I've been having visions of myself—in the future, I think—and I hate what I see."

"Wind, stop." He drew up short, and I had to jog back and stop in front of him. Damn it. The face-to-face conversation was about to commence.

"Okay, tell me what you're talking about. You don't usually leave room for interpretation, and you're being vague here," he said.

"I'm seeing myself, Michael." I took a deep breath. "I'm all skinny and washed up and working the Tilt-A-Whirl at some ocean amusement park. A boardwalk, I think. It's really me. I can see my face, my eyes, and it's me." I sounded like I was pleading with him. What was I pleading for? For it to not be true? For it to be normal? For him to say something that would make sense of these visions? Yes, that's what I wanted.

"How many visions have you had?" Now that's more like it—take charge like the research scientist you are, man.

"Five, I think." I rubbed my arms, not wanting to lose the heat of our warm-up run. The dry leaves chattered in the breeze.

"Five, okay. Have they been the same?"

"No. But I'm always the same. I mean, I am always worn out, old, tired."

"Tired? Have you been feeling okay, healthy, lately?"

"Yeah," I told him. Actually, I had been feeling a little stressed out, if I let myself admit it. With the new classes, the training of my graduate assistants, the speech for my mother, Guadalupe's health and Asha's proposal—yeah, I'd have to admit I might be stressed out.

His eyes searched my face, looking for clues to disprove my last answer.

"Maybe that's it." I rubbed my forehead between my eyebrows. It felt good, like rubbing away a stain. "I have had a lot going on."

"You're a scientist. You're not used to having things happen that you can't explain—that fact is probably stressing you out even more," he offered.

"Yeah," I said, "I can see that." And I could. These visions had turned me into a suspension bridge with one end anchored in today and the other end in, possibly, a dismal future.

"Windler, that might be it, but will you let me know?"

"Yeah, thanks for listening," I said and smiled up at him. Sweat was giving up the fight of hanging on to the ends of his black curls. He wiped the back of his hand across his forehead and smiled back at me.

"Anytime."

"Let's run," I said, and we did.

CHAPTER TWELVE

Shove

"Excuse me, Dr. Windler." A stylishly dressed woman I'd never met before was picking her way down the deep stairs in the lecture hall. The steps were oddly spaced to accommodate each new level holding a row of desks, so making one's way down them for the first time was usually an affair one had to pay attention to. This woman's kitten heels and tight knee-length skirt made the going just that much more difficult. Her black swing coat moved left-to-right-to-left again as she reached for handholds on the backs of the chairs.

"Good morning," I called up to her. My Monday lecture class had just ended, and a few students were still chatting on the perimeter of the large room. A quiet student named Virginia was facing me, standing alone near the front row, with her Louis Vuitton backpack thrown over one shoulder and her body twisted half around to watch the approach of the woman. Had she been about to ask me about something? I looked at her and asked, "Virginia, were you going to talk to me about something?" This student had never interacted much with me, and it would be a pity for her to finally need something from me and be interrupted by someone else.

"No, I…no," she stammered, "but my mom wants to talk to you."

"Your mom?"

"Yeah," Virginia said as she motioned to the woman who'd made her way to the bottom of the room and was now standing beside Virginia. Ah, I could see the likeness in their waxed eyebrows and in their perfectly upturned noses. Perhaps they shared the same cosmetic surgeon. Was mom interested in become a student? Or was she perhaps interested in supporting the U in some financial way? Alumni and parents of students often made donations to various departments or events like the "Science at the U" film series. She certainly looked like she had some spare cash to offer.

"Hello." She extended a well-manicured hand to me. I shook it. "I'm Courtney Marsdale, Virginia's mother."

"Good morning." I repeated my greeting from a few moments ago.

"I guess I'll cut straight to the chase here," Courtney Marsdale said, and I got the distinct impression that she was not going to be offering her support in any way. In fact, I got the impression she was going to be less than supportive.

"Okay," I said.

"Virginia has always been an 'A' student. In your class…well, you are not giving Virginia an 'A,' and this has never happened before." She eyed me through lids that were half-closed.

This was the reason she showed up in my classroom? Seriously?

"Ms. Marsdale?" I began. "I don't give students grades. Students earn their grades."

"Well, certainly, you must be the person to grade the students' work—you are the instructor, after all, right?" she asked. Her tone brought my mother's face to mind.

"Yes, I score the work," I said. "We've had five labs and two exams. Each lab grade is very objective—based on procedures, outcomes and notes. The two exams are also objectively graded.

There's nothing subjective about the grade Virginia has earned in this course." I talked fast because I had the gut feeling that this woman wanted to cut me short.

"Virginia's grade is unacceptable," Ms. Marsdale said. "Perhaps an error was made in the grading of her lab work or her exams?" I looked at her. Her blue eyes held no shame or recognition that this encounter was unusual. When I didn't answer, she continued, "There must be an extra credit opportunity available to her?"

"Virginia," I turned to address my student, "are you concerned about your grade in this course?"

She toyed with her backpack strap. A few seconds passed before she answered, "Not really."

"Do you know how you earned the grade you have?" I asked. Was I really having this conversation? I felt suddenly like a middle-school teacher.

"Of course I do," she said. She looked embarrassed that the conversation was taking place. It occurred to me that mommy was probably the one who had had this idea, not Virginia. A very entitled mommy who was used to getting whatever she wanted.

"Virginia, I have office hours printed out on the syllabus I gave you the first day of the course. They are also available to you on the course website. Will you find a time to meet with me so we can discuss how you can improve your grade with the next lab and the final exam?" I cut mommy out of the discussion. I couldn't blame her for wanting good things for her daughter, but, seriously? Maybe I was being hypercritical because my mother would never have gone to bat for me like this. Or maybe I felt an intense dislike for this woman because she did remind me of my mother. At any rate, I was going to create a lie in order to cut this impromptu meeting short.

"I'm sorry, Ms. Marsdale," I began, "I have a meeting with a graduate student and her thesis committee. I have to run. But don't worry, Virginia and I will meet to discuss her grade." I couldn't help myself from putting emphasis on the fact that it was Virginia's grade.

I turned, scooped up my lecture notes and phone and bounded up the stairs, not caring how awkward it looked from behind. I had never run up these stairs before, and it made me laugh out loud to be tackling them like this. My giant monster steps left Virginia and her mom in the lecture hall, which would only be empty for about another five minutes. Basic Economics would be starting soon, so Virginia wouldn't feel the heat too long before they were interrupted by the instructor and students.

When I got to my office, I slipped in and closed the door gently behind me. I did not want to be followed by this mother and her kid. Then I thought, why prolong any agony? If she were coming for more discussion, it would happen sooner or later. If they found me here, I could always say the committee had postponed by a few minutes. I took my glasses off and rubbed my forehead. Seriously. A mom? Maybe I'd pin Virginia's grade to her coat collar for her mom to find when Virginia came home to do laundry next weekend. Ugh. I leaned back in my chair and closed my eyes for a tired moment...

The back of my head was nearly parallel to the tabletop. My posture made me look tired and old. The straps of my tank top had stretched to the point of almost being useless, which was perhaps why I had on a once-white lifeguard-style tank top on beneath it. I watched myself breathe shallowly at the table, my head in my hands.

A loud, ornery bellowing blasted from another room, and I watched the back of my head snap up, a soldier coming to attention. The yelling must have alarmed me because I lost no time standing, pushing my chair in silently and turning in the small kitchen to the sink of dirty dishes. I twisted the faucet and let my fingers test the temperature. The bellowing again. Not fast enough with the dishes and no beer and nothing good on TV without cable, and you better not be reading another goddamned book. I watched my lips as they lost color and pressed into a thin line. I heard myself say nothing as I rubbed the space between my eyebrows.

"Look, if I have to get myself a beer, there's gonna be..." A deep voice mumbled, becoming increasingly louder, or closer, from around the kitchen wall's corner. A shirtless mass of stringy muscle walked into the small kitchen. Axel. He opened the fridge door, peered in, slammed the door and turned slowly and menacingly to me. The back of me trembled once before he smashed the front of my shoulders with his open palms. With a resounding smack, the base of my head met the edge of the counter on my way down. I watched myself slide out of view on the other side of the counter.

"You're worthless," he bellowed. "We're outta beer. What the fuck?"

"Axel," I heard my voice, quiet and unsteady as I put a hand above me on the counter to pull myself up off the floor. "Ax, you said you were going to get it." The man put his booted foot against my collarbone and forced me to remain on the floor. He was no longer sexy. He was scary. He grabbed a fistful of my hair and pulled me halfway off the floor. I scrambled to get my legs underneath me. Before I was able to support myself and stand, he let go off my hair and let me drop back to the linoleum. I heard myself cry out. He kicked me in the ribs, halfheartedly, thank goodness.

"Stay there because that's where you belong," he spat at me as I lay in the fetal position on the floor.

I opened my eyes and, feeling the need to vomit, searched for my office wastepaper basket. It was tucked halfway under my desk. Between heaves, I heard a tapping at the mostly closed door.

"Are you okay, Cassie? I'm coming in," Art announced a moment before I felt his hand making small circles on my upper back. His hands then swept my hair away from my face, which still hovered over the wastepaper basket. I started crying.

CHAPTER THIRTEEN

Beaujolais Nouveau

Sunny's small kitchen counter was festooned with unopened bottles of Beaujolais Nouveau. The colorful labels ran the gamut from a humble pencil sketching to the garish glittery sort. Our primary mission of this evening was, as usual for a Thirsty Thursday, to enjoy each other's company and drink wine. Our secondary mission, however, was special tonight since this was the third Thursday of November, Beaujolais Nouveau night. Tonight we were going to vote on this year's best Beaujolais Nouveau. No doubt, we'd also be toasting again (and again) the fact that Minnesota voters had defeated a proposal to insert a ban on same-sex marriage in the state's constitution.

It was a week before Thanksgiving, and Asha and I were planning on spending the holiday with Guadalupe in the hospital. Guadalupe had not grown up with Thanksgiving as a child, but she fully embraced any food-oriented celebration. It wouldn't be the same this year; that was for certain. I had been down for days over the fact that Guadalupe wouldn't be able to indulge in turkey, pumpkin pie or the usual merriment, so I was especially hell-bent on enjoying the Beaujolais festivities.

Now I eyed the wines and thought about how the new grapes of the summer had been squashed down into the bottles of wine before us. France had had a long, dry, hot one this year, so the wine had promise. The summer before had been a cold, rainy one and the grapes had offered little in the way of flavor. Last year's Beaujolais Nouveau had been a letdown. But this year...well, we had hope.

"Let's get these opened, so that they can breathe a bit," Whitney said as she held and inspected the bottle with the pencil sketch label. "What vineyard is this one from? I've never seen this label before."

"Okay, I cheated on that one," Jenn confessed. "It's a Californian—"

"Ohh, come on," Asha moaned. "You've gotta play by the rules!"

"I did! I tried," Jenn defended herself, "I mean, well...it's a Californian Beaujolais-styled wine. Still this year's grapes, see?" Jenn pointed to the vintage on the label. I looked. It appeared as if it could have been written by any of us, but then again, the whole label looked that way.

"Okay, but if this wine wins," Asha said, "we're going with the top two—it'll be a tie. Deal?"

"Deal," Jenn agreed.

"Whit, the corkscrews are in the top drawer, on the left. Should be three of them," Sunny directed from the other room. She was laying out cheese, fruit and other delectables for us on her dining table, which, due to the tiny nature of her apartment, was in the living room.

"Seriously?" Jenn hollered back to Sunny. "Seriously, Sun? Your pad is this...petite, and you have room for *three* corkscrews?"

Sunny came and leaned against the kitchen's doorframe and asked, "How do you think I cope with living in such a small space? One must be properly, continually lubricated to squeeze through such small passages." She smiled devilishly.

"Eww...!" Jenn laughed.

"That's not what I was talking about!" Sunny exclaimed. I laughed. I knew that Sunny only drank on Thirsty Thursdays. She had told me a few months ago that she was going to try to start remembering to drink more often so that our monthly gatherings didn't hit her as hard. She said she was going to increase her tolerance. And then last month she confessed, when I asked how her drinking project was coming along, that she just plain forgot to drink. She enjoyed it, she claimed, but she never remembered to open a bottle when she was on her own.

The gentle pop of the first cork being eased out brought a cheer from the seven of us. Esme had not yet arrived, but Jenn, Sunny, Whitney, Asha, Cory, Anna and I were all ready to start sampling and rating this year's wine. None of us had any qualifications to actually rate wine, of course. This was just for fun. The way it worked was that we'd bring as many different bottles as we could find of the Beaujolais Nouveau, which only had a shelf life of a few months due to the way it was processed. It was meant to be enjoyed over the holidays, but not much beyond New Year. This year, so far, we had wines from seven different vineyards, including the Californian. We had a few duplicates from several vineyards, and that was a good thing in case any of them wound up being a favorite.

The hostess provided cards on which we could make notes on each wine and rate the wines we sampled, swilled or slammed. At the end of the evening, the cards would be collected, results would be tallied and a victor would be crowned. If you happened to be the lucky individual who brought the winning vineyard's wine to the party, you were crowned the year's Beaujolais Nouveau Goddess. Last year, Whitney, Asha and Esme shared the title, all three having brought the winning wine from Georges Deboeuf's vineyard. Their title is forever immortalized in the Beaujolais Nouveau photo album that gets passed from hostess to hostess. In the picture they are smiling with mouths stained purple from the wine, holding up their bottles and wearing crowns made out of printer paper.

This year I had brought a couple bottles from Joseph Drouhin, and Asha was trying her luck again with the Deboeuf. Sunny had her bases covered with a Deboeuf, a Jean Bererd & Fils and a Drouhin. Looked like I'd be sharing the title, if I won, which made me happy because I didn't really want to pose alone, sporting a paper crown and holding a wine bottle for the camera. The second cork was eased out, there was another cheer, less robust than the first, and then the intercom for the downstairs door buzzed.

"I got it," I called. I was closest to the intercom, which was beside the kitchen window. That seemed like a funny place for it, but then as I got close enough to the intercom, I saw the sense it made. Out the window, I could see Esme at the front door below me. She was standing in the hazy pool of golden light cast by the front door's ancient chandelier, and she was decked out in a wash of tropical colors made even brighter by the surrounding drabness of the November night. She held a cardboard box. I buzzed her up and then realized she might not be able to open the door with her arms that full. I couldn't buzz the door open and get down to help her in time.

"Sunny, Esme needs help at the door—her arms are full!" I called out. Sunny and Cory were the only two who weren't crammed into the minute kitchen. Nurse Anna, Sunny's girlfriend, was actually perched on what was left of the small counter space in order to make room for us all to be in there.

"I got her," Sunny hollered on her way out of the apartment.

Anna leaned over from her countertop seat to peer out of the window, "What are her arms full of—oh! She brought a whole case!"

"Looks like it," I said as Anna and I pressed our heads together to see downstairs. "She has high hopes for us tonight, I guess," I said. We saw Sunny swing the door open for Esme, try to take the case of wine from her arms and then stop trying to help. It appeared they were talking because little wisps of steamy breath floated out around their heads. Sunny had to stand with her hip against the door to keep it propped open.

They were still talking, standing on the top step just outside the building's entrance. Then Sunny's hands flew up to cup both sides of Esme's face. It looked like she was wiping tears away from her cheeks.

"Oh no…" Anna breathed, steaming up the window and our view. She wiped the window dry with her sleeve, and we continued to spy on Sunny and Esme below us. Esme finally relinquished the box of wine, and Sunny placed it on the top step inside the open door so that she could wrap her arms around Esme and hold her.

"Ohhh…something bad has happened," I said just loudly enough for Anna to hear over the chatter around us. We saw Esme and Sunny sit down on the top step; Sunny kept one arm around Esme, and Esme covered her face with her hands, crying, I thought. She was rocking back and forth, and Sunny was talking, or comforting, in little steamy puffs. I felt tears prick at the corners of my eyes.

"I bet it's that bitch Elizabeth," Anna said quietly. "Sorry!" She turned her head slightly to see my reaction.

"No, no need, I bet you're right!" I answered. "Let's go help bring them up." But we weren't in a good place to move easily to the apartment's door, so I motioned for Asha's attention. She was the closest person to the door.

"Can you go down and help Esme and Sunny?" I asked loudly over the cheerful hubbub. "Esme's crying on the front step…" All of the talking and laughing stopped. As a whole and almost as if we'd practiced, everyone turned and walked, rather quickly, out of the apartment. We trampled down the staircase toward the front door.

"What happened?" Asha, beside me, asked as we descended.

"I don't know," I answered.

"Elizabeth, probably," Jenn retorted sourly from just a few paces in front of us.

We all blasted out the open front door together and apparently shocked Esme and Sunny, who were still talking softly on the top step.

"*Mon dieu!*" Esme cried out, jumping a little where she sat.

"Oh! Oh! Oh…okay," Sunny responded to the mass of us. "Everything's okay, Esme's okay," Sunny said, but her look said something else. Her lips were pursed and her eyes were narrowed as she looked up at us over the shoulder of her arm that was still wrapped around Esme. Suddenly Sunny's face opened up, and she asked, "You guys didn't let my apartment door close, did you?"

For the next thirty-five minutes, we sat in the hallway outside of Sunny's apartment door. As we waited for the building's superintendent to bring us a spare key, we listened to Esme tell of Elizabeth's escapades with not one, not two, but three other women. From the way the story unfolded, it seemed that Elizabeth had a thing for other women's women. Each of the three she'd been sleeping with for the past two or three months, behind Esme's back, were in what appeared to be committed relationships.

"Goes to show, you just never know," Whitney said.

"No, sometimes you do just know," Jenn countered.

"Jenn? This coming from you? Player of he year?" Esme teased. I was glad to see that she felt a little better after having talked it through with us.

"Right," Jenn said, "but sometimes you do know. You just know that it's only these two people and no one else, you know? Besides, I've never slept with someone who was committed to anyone else."

"Maybe not committed, no," Cory said, "but maybe in a 'committed relationship'?"

"No, seriously," Jenn said and shook her head. "I hope not anyway! Maybe you really do never really know…or don't ever know…or whatever!" Things got quiet for a few moments.

"Player of the year? Really?" Jenn finally asked.

"Yes!" the rest of us said in unison. Jenn grinned and looked proud of herself.

The conversation turned to Whitney's biological daughter dilemma. The daughter she'd given up for adoption when she was fifteen was still emailing her, only now Whitney was emailing back. They had exchanged six long emails so far, and

Whitney felt the kid was pretty normal, just curious about her biological mother.

The name of the girl—or young woman, really—was Helena, and she lived in a small town in Wisconsin. Whitney said it didn't sound like she was in a bad place. Helena had graduated from a university in Ashland, Wisconsin, five years ago, and now she owned and operated her own preschool. Helena had written nice things about her adoptive parents and had said she had a good childhood.

Cory had been watching Whitney's face with so much love and support glowing from her that I had to send out a silent thank you for her staying with Whit, her newish girlfriend, through all of this.

"Get this," Cory interjected, "she has a lesbian partner named, of all things, Cory!" She laughed with joy and leaned back against the hallway wall. She threw her hands up in the air and said, "So we know she must have good taste in women!"

"Yes, she must have good taste," Asha laughed with her.

"Wait," I asked, "so she's a lesbian?"

"Yup," Whitney said. She put her hand on Cory's bent knee and shook it gently. "And thanks to Cory here, I am getting through all of this just fine." Cory wrapped her in half a bear hug and kissed her on the cheek. I could hear Esme's breathing catch in her throat. Oh, seeing the love was going to be too much for her. Esme put her hands up to her face. She was crying again.

"Ohhh…" she sobbed. "Oh, I want my own Cory so badly!"

I put my hand on her leg and patted her. We all looked at each other. I'm guessing my face was as long as everyone else's. The building superintendent chose that moment to bound up the stairs and let us into Sunny's apartment.

"Come on, Es." I patted her thigh. "Come on inside." I squatted next to her.

"*Ouais, chouchou*, I need to pull myself together," she said, wiping her eyes and standing up.

"I got the box," Cory said as Esme bent down to pick it up.

"Thank you." Esme's voice was still shaky.

"Esme, why the whole case?" Cory asked as she peeked under one of the box's cardboard flaps after she hoisted it to one hip. "Oh, it's twelve different bottles!"

Esme wailed, "I just really, really need to be the Beaujolais Nouveau Goddess tonight!" She laughed through her few lingering tears, and Cory and I laughed with her.

"We'll make sure of it!" I declared. I followed them in, thinking about whether one can really never be sure or not. The world was teeming with both Corys and with Elizabeths. If we could be certain of nothing else in this world, at least we could count on that.

CHAPTER FOURTEEN

Memorial Advice

"Michael, can I ask you something?"

We were in the lab on the Sunday night following Thanksgiving. The thermostat had gone on the fritz over the long weekend, and we'd been texted by maintenance that a water pipe had burst due to the sudden drop in temperature. Even though we were told the lab had been cleaned up, we'd decided to come in to make sure everything was ready for Monday's classes.

"You just did," Michael said and laughed at his own joke. I threw the lab towel I was drying the counter with at him. He swiped it out of the air before it hit him.

"Look, ass, I'm serious here." I was crabby and sad and didn't need any of his shit right now.

Guadalupe had died two nights before, in the hospital, alone. Asha and I had sat with Guadalupe on Thanksgiving night. Lupe had been so pale that I'd been able to watch the lavender veins under her eyes slowly pulse. I knew it wouldn't be long, so I went to see her the following night, just prior to her death. She had slipped into a coma earlier that afternoon. The nurses said all I could do was sit by her bed and talk to her in case she could hear me.

I had told her about the visions I was having. When she offered no reaction, I told her about Asha and my upcoming unlawful wedding. I thanked her for giving me the love that kept me going as a child, as a teen and finally as an adult. She didn't say anything, but I felt her warmth in my heart, telling me it had all been her pleasure.

"Okay, I'm sorry, Wind, I'm sorry," Michael said as he shook out the towel, set it on the counter and came around to put his hand on my shoulder. He shook me gently and dipped his head down to smile into my eyes. "I'm sorry. What?"

"I'm speaking at Guadalupe's memorial service on Thursday, and I wanted to know if there's anything…special I should do or know," I said. Michael was a church-goer, so I figured he'd have some advice for me.

Michael's expression showed he was trying to decide between two reactions.

"Are you asking me this," he chose to ask, "because I'm Mexican, and you think I'll have some secret insight on what you should do at your Mexican nanny's funeral?" Michael clowned with a big grin and waggling eyebrows. "Is this a Mexican thing?"

I stared at him. Jesus. What an asswipe. I'd asked him the question because he'd been raised Catholic and I didn't want to screw things up and disrespect Lupe's religion. It's not like my family had ever spent much time together in church. I picked up my backpack from the lab counter and walked out of the room.

"Wait, Windler, I'm just playing," he called out.

I turned to look at him, smiling and nodding his head, encouraging me to feel the humor in the quip he had just thrown at me.

"Fuck you, fucker," I said. I turned and left.

* * *

Asha wiped her hands on the dishtowel and came over to stand behind me at the breakfast bar. She said nothing as she rubbed my shoulders and pressed her lips to the back of my head. I took my glasses off and set them on the counter. I let my head settle on my crossed arms on the bar and felt the tears begin to slide down my nose.

"What can I do, Cassie?" she murmured into my hair.

"Nothing, just make me feel alive, Asha," I sniffled, standing up and turning to face her.

"I will," she responded. She kissed me gently on the lips, playing with time as if there had been no urgency in my request. I parted her lips, impatient, with the tip of my tongue, and when she responded in no hurry with her own tongue, I decided that things would have to be stepped up a notch in order to take my mind off Guadalupe, Michael and anything else that might be stressing me into hallucinations.

I kept entertaining her mouth while I began undoing her belt and trousers. Such funny pants she wore, all 1940s' menswear, not quite Annie Hall, but close, without the flair. They did fall to the floor like any other trousers would, that was for certain. Asha stepped out of the pool of pants and kicked them aside.

"Good idea…but I think it's more about you right now," she said against my mouth. I didn't protest. I usually thought fifty-fifty was the way to go, with a little something for both of us, but right now, I needed two things. One: a big distraction. Two: to feel close to Asha. Looked like it was going to be all me for a few moments.

Asha pulled my shirt up over my head, melded her lips to mine, removed my bra without breaking off our kiss and slid her hands over my naked breasts. She pressed her mouth once more hard against mine before trailing softer kisses down my neck to my shoulder to my nipple. Waves rippled all the way to the center of my body, and I could feel myself begin to get bigger for the want of her touch. I sighed, and she mmmm'ed against my throat before turning me around to face the breakfast bar. She ran her fingertips from the nape of my neck down to the top of my jeans and then around my hips to unzip and push open my fly. Cold fire followed her touch. Her fingertips grazed my belly, and a shiver tortured me. Was she trying to kill me with this lackadaisical speed?

"Asha, come on," I pleaded, pressing back into her hips. I was already throbbing against the seam of my jeans, and I so wanted *her* to be there, not some wedge of denim, when I finished. I pushed my jeans off over my hips and stepped them down and off one leg at a time. I heard Asha chuckle behind me, but I felt too good to take it personally. I may have actually chuckled myself at that point.

"Come on," I repeated, pulling her hand around to the front of my panties. Damn. The panties. I pushed them down too until they were reunited with my jeans on the floor. Asha finally picked up on my urgency. She pushed my shoulders gently down until I was lying over the breakfast bar, my cheek and breasts pressed to the cold granite.

"Yes," I hissed. Her whole hand gripped me between my legs and I pushed hard into her palm. She let me build a little like that until she thought I was ready for a bit more concentrated attention. Her cool fingertips balanced themselves on one point, playing there like a car about to crash over the crushed guardrail at the side of a cliff. One passenger shifts this way to keep the car roadside; one hand placed atop the steering wheel causes the car to teeter further over the edge, one "Oh My God" from an innocent bystander and wheeeeeeeee! The car is propelled at breakneck speed toward its final resting place. But just as the ground is getting closer and closer through the windshield, in jumps another passenger! Asha thrust into me at just the right moment to keep that car crashing. God, she was perfect with her timing. I felt myself clutch her fingers, grinding my hips forward, the back of her hand probably mashed against the cupboard in front of me. As the spasms began to subside, I felt her withdraw and then slide in again just enough to send two more quivers through my body.

I went limp against the breakfast bar and Asha slowly pulled herself from inside of me. Her other hand, however, she kept pressed firmly to my pubic bone, knowing that I wouldn't want her to take that one from me just yet. I tried to pick my head up off the granite, but I felt so delicious that I had to ask myself what the point was. I lay there for a moment longer. Asha kissed along the tops of my shoulders. I felt her small breasts through her shirt against my back and started thinking about returning the favor.

"How was that?" she asked.

"No one survived," I reported.

She chuckled and asked if that was a good thing. I told her in this case it was a very good thing.

"It sure was quick," she teased.

"Oh, really?" I tried to sound put out. "And let's see how long you can last," I teased back, prying my cheek from the counter and turning on her. She play-shrieked and ran from the room in the direction of the staircase. I gave chase and, being a runner and all, I caught up with her.

CHAPTER FIFTEEN

Eulogizing Lupe

The gas pedal shook hands with the floor mat. I introduced them only because I thought we were going to be late, but when I pulled into the parking lot at 229 Mississippi Curve, otherwise known as Saint Maria's Blessed Heart Church, there were only two other cars parked there, and one had FTHR JO personalized plates. My heart dropped, thinking that it was going to be a small turnout. Asha checked my phone to be sure that we were at the right church. Almost as soon as she had verified it, a tall, thin priest walked out of a wooden door off the church's foyer and greeted us warmly.

Turns out, Asha and I were an hour and fifteen minutes early. Guadalupe was laughing somewhere, I was certain. The priest, Father Joseph, smiled down at us and asked if we'd like to sit with Guadalupe's ashes while we waited for the ceremony to begin. I thought that sounded perfect, but I couldn't do more than nod and swallow the saltwater that was suddenly trickling down the back of my throat.

"Thank you. We'd like that," Asha said.

She took my hand, and we followed Father Joseph. Guadalupe was in a small, surprisingly small, wooden box that was covered in carvings. Ivy encircled flowers and birds around the middle of her box. My father had asked me what she might appreciate most on it, and I had thought that some aspect of nature would make her happy. He had done well in his selection.

I touched the wooden etchings on the lid and was surprised that it was warm. My fingers flew to press my lips, which had pursed of their own accord. I laughed then because I realized that was the most textbook reaction I could have had to a warm ash box. But really, why was it warm? I touched the box again, and this time I left my fingers there for a long time. *Hi, Guadalupe. Hi.* I closed my eyes.

I pictured Guadalupe, from when I first remembered her. Her long black hair was glossy and thick, and I was forever begging her to let me braid it, unbraid it and braid it again. Her skin was so wonderful, brown and smooth, and her arms were like vises around me every day after school, letting me know she'd always be there, that she chose to be there, that she chose me. I kept my eyes closed.

I breathed in, trying to capture any particles of Guadalupe that might be floating around me. I smelled incense and wax, but Lupe must be in the air as well, I thought. I breathed in, kept my eyes closed and relaxed my forehead, which I could feel was all drawn up and tensed. The sound of my own breathing was accompanied by a woman's voice, warm and familiar...

I couldn't place the voice. I opened my eyes, not to what I'd expected, but to a very different tableau.

"She chose to take the baby that was in the air," said the woman with the familiar, but unidentifiable voice. A much, much older version of me, she looked solemn as she spoke. She was holding the worn-out me, the one I was now getting used to seeing in these visions, by the shoulders. The younger woman started crying. She pressed her hands to her eyes, winced and dragged her hands and her tears across her angular cheekbones into her hair, which she pulled back taut on each side of her face. She held fistfuls of the coppery strands as if causing herself this pain might replace the other ache. Her left eye showed the yellow-gray remnants of a bruise.

It was only a few seconds before she released her hair, then her breath and met the older woman's gaze again.

"Why didn't you tell me before now?" my voice, with its unusual drawl, asked.

"Sweetheart, I didn't think I would ever tell, but today…I thought of their nanny, I thought of her tears and you've been so sad…," the older woman said. "I just thought you should know. I wanted you to know you're not alone."

"I feel alone."

"I know." The older woman moved to capture my shoulders in her arm. She pressed her hand to my face and her lips to the side of my head. "I know," she said again.

I felt such despair and fear that I thought I might collapse. I felt as if there was no place I could find safety, not even there, where I expected to find it. My heart could cave in, and I'd have been better off if it had, but now, this news, why now? My heart ached for the one woman who'd loved me like a mother. What if I did have someone else in this world? Someone safe. What if…

"Cassie?" Asha whispered. I heard it as an echo. Had she had to say my name more than once? "Cassie, are you all right? You've gone pale."

What did the woman mean, I was not alone? I inhaled deeply, trying to ground myself. This vision was different. I'd felt a much stronger connection…I mean, I'd actually *felt* it. If these visions, these episodes, were indeed brought on by stress, as Michael and I had guessed earlier, maybe Guadalupe's death was going to be the event that pushed me right over the edge of my sanity. Maybe this wasn't my future that I was seeing but just some multiple-personality angle I was using to try to cope with my life. That thought scared the hell out of me. That couldn't be it, could it? Christ, anything would be better than that. A brain tumor. Couldn't brain tumors cause visions? Let it be a brain tumor…that would at least allow me to deal with it.

As I stood before Guadalupe's mourners later, I tried to concentrate on expressing how fortunate I was to have had

Lupe in my life, but the scene and the intense feelings that had accompanied it were nearly impossible to shake off. Who was the new woman, the older one who looked so much like me? She was too old to be a long-lost sister. Maybe an auntie? I turned my eyes to my mother in the front pew. I examined her platinum-blond hair, icy blue eyes and petite frame. The new woman didn't resemble her much at all. And she was almost the complete opposite of my father with his tall build, almost black hair, dark eyes and olive complexion. She was an unlikely candidate, then, to be related to either one of them. Who could she be?

I slid my eyes off my father and onto Asha. She smiled at me and nodded, probably coaxing me to go on with what I had been saying. Asha had on a black suit and a crisp, pale pink shirt that she had buttoned all the way to the base of her throat. As usual, the left side of her hair had a few wayward scruffs sticking out. I loved her look. She managed, as usual, to look formal in an offhand way, casual, yet perfectly put together. A woman near the back of the church cleared her throat and sniffled. I attempted to let the vision go for a moment so that I could continue with Guadalupe's eulogy.

"So, Guadalupe was family to me. *Así, Guadalupe fue familia me*. At our table, while she was teaching me to read Spanish and I was teaching her to read English, she was like a mother to me, *fue como una madre me*."

I said this without making eye contact with anyone, especially with my mother. Guadalupe had been mother to me more than my own mother ever was, but I still didn't want to feel as if I were throwing the fact in my mother's face. Instead I looked at Guadalupe's family members who'd made the trip from Mexico to be here and to take Guadalupe's ashes home with them. They nodded to let me know that they either understood my attempt at Spanish or they understood what I was saying about her.

"At the Saints ball games, Guadalupe was like a sister to me. She never once showed up without her Saints baseball cap. She never once said 'no' to gluttonous amounts of ballpark junk food. And she never once said 'no' to accompanying me."

Now it was I who cleared my throat and sniffled. I made eye contact with Whitney, who was sitting between Sunny and Jenn. She smiled sadly at me. The three of them looked like little penguins, all polar and comical in their black jackets and bright white shirts. On second thought, maybe they looked more like nuns lined up in the pew than penguins mucking about on an ice cap. Esme, seated beside Jenn, was closer to the equator with her outfit, a tropical mélange of color and texture. Her golden hoop earrings dangled all the way down to her shoulders. Her headscarf was black.

"I'm not an overly religious person, and I don't know what it takes to become a proper saint, but I do think it fitting that my mind's favorite image of Guadalupe is of her beautiful face beaming at me from under a Saints cap."

Michael, sitting next to Asha, nodded his head and wiped his eyes with a handkerchief. I was surprised he had one. I was happy he had it, though, because at that point he had a need for one. He blew his nose in it. I waited for his honk to subside before concluding.

"I will miss Guadalupe terribly, as I know you will, and I am so glad you all came here today to pay tribute to her."

As I left the pulpit, Father Joseph caught me with a brief, firm hug and a whispered thank you. He walked to the second row to usher Rosa Moreno, one of Guadalupe's friends, to the pulpit as I slid into the space Michael and Asha created for me between them. Asha took my hand in hers and squeezed it. Michael whispered to me that I did a nice job and honked into his handkerchief one last time before Rosa started telling us about meeting Guadalupe for the first time at Novak Park. She called the first meeting "The Nanny Connection," and she shared how she and Guadalupe teased each other about the very close resemblances they shared with their "children."

I laughed with everyone else and glanced over my shoulder at Grace and Lucas Wintersmith. Grace had accompanied me through most every class that had an alphabetical seating chart. We were locker neighbors throughout our four years of high school. Grace was looking down now, but Lucas smiled at me, his green eyes crinkling at the corners. I smiled back, thinking about how Rosa and Lupe must have laughed their heads off over the resemblances, or lack thereof, among the two towheaded, light-eyed Wintersmiths, dark strawberry-blond, green-eyed me, and their young, brown-skinned, black-haired selves.

For all the oppression the young nannies must have experienced, I was glad that they had had each other as friends to buffer the bad and celebrate the good. And with my mother being who she was—well, I knew that there would have been a good deal of bad for Guadalupe to tolerate. My father, for his part, had been compassionate and kind toward her, but my mother had never given much thought to anyone else's needs, so, in word and deed, she had treated Guadalupe as little more than a second-class citizen, someone to take for granted.

I'm so sorry, Lupe. I'm sorry. Thank you for putting up with it all to stay with me. Thank you.

* * *

"How are you doing, Cassie?" my father asked me after the service. He put his arm around my shoulder and pulled me gently into his side. He'd arranged to have caterers provide everyone with a luncheon in the church's small but pretty common area. I looked at the delicate cakes and the sterling coffee service and wondered how many of my parents' actions were shows for others.

"I'm okay. You?"

"Did you get to spend some time with her at the hospital?" My father released my shoulder so he could look me in the eyes. His eyes were tired, as if he'd been carrying a burden too big for one person. Had he been crying? He wasn't much of a crier, preferring to bottle his emotions while asking about how others were feeling instead. He was less into show than my mother, that was for certain, but I still felt at times that he gave in to appearances. This was not one of those times. He was genuinely grieving the passing of Guadalupe.

"Dad, how come you didn't speak?" I had thought he would share some stories with us all.

"I decided to let those who knew Guadalupe best do the talking today," he said, adjusting his tie to a more comfortable, but imperceptible, looseness. He pulled out a chair for me, so I sat down. He sat in the chair beside me.

"You knew her," I prompted.

"No, Cassie, I don't think I knew her as well as others who spoke about her today knew her," he said, shaking his head. "I was remiss in not getting to know her as a person; she was more of an employee to me." He was sad about that. I was sad that he was sad. Here he was, in his suit that cost him more than Guadalupe's entire wardrobe, feeling sad that he didn't know her better. There wasn't anything I could do to make him feel better about it, but I still found myself wishing that I could take away at least some of his sorrow. His hands were folded on the table in front of him, and I placed one of my hands over the knuckly knot his had created.

Across the room, I saw Michael, Asha and Jenn waiting behind two women to get coffees. Michael was holding out the handkerchief, and Asha was shaking her head and holding up her hand, declining the proffered scrap of linen. Jenn was laughing. Ah. The handkerchief must have been one of Asha's to begin with. That made more sense.

I said nothing to my father about his lack of knowledge of Guadalupe but thought of the time that I scolded Wasabi for eating a monarch butterfly in our backyard. She'd been chasing it, taking furry jabs at it as it fluttered by.

This lasted for long moments before she caught it in one paw, brought it to her whiskered mouth and began munching it. I hadn't thought she'd actually catch it, but when she did, I bellowed, "Nooo…!" She'd gone from sitting up straight, proudly devouring the prey she'd skillfully bagged, to scrunched up and finishing off the insect like a beggar who'd just stolen yesterday's bread crust. It had taken me a couple of seconds to realize that I'd just crushed the mighty hunter's joy. When I did, I went overboard with making a big deal out of what a good job she'd done, admiring the uneaten wings left as trophies and oohing and ahhing over her prowess.

I thought now about how I never cared when Wasabi ate little spiders and moths, but when it came to the butterfly, it was a different story. Why did I feel more pain for the eaten monarch than I did for the multitude of devoured gray moths and spiders? Was I more like my mother and father than I assumed I was?

"Actually, Cass," my father continued, "I have been remiss in many things." He looked at me as if he had something else to say, but he spoke no further. We sat quietly for a few moments just watching others as they consoled each other or smiled quietly over shared stories.

"Here, Wind. Here, Dr. Windler. Thought you two could use it," Michael, with Asha at his elbow, set down two coffees in front of my father and me. I didn't say thank you because I was still sore about him asking me if my asking him for eulogy guidance was "a Mexican thing," but I did take a sip of the coffee. Turning to take the coffees Asha was holding, he set them on the table as my father stood up to pull out a chair for Asha. It made me feel good to see him being polite to her. He had never offered much positive energy in her direction, but, that being said, he'd never directed much negative energy at her either. The same couldn't be said for my mother, who was noticeably absent from the table. She was filling her time talking animatedly with Grace and Lucas Wintersmith's father.

I had hung up on her in the middle of a high-pitched tirade the night before in which she listed reasons Asha should not attend Guadalupe's memorial service. Now her shrill laughter shocked its way through the room. I started at the sound and looked at her. She was reaching out to touch the wrist of Mr. Wintersmith, and she was laughing like glass breaking. Mr. Wintersmith looked uncomfortable, as did a few other people near them. I watched as his eyes sought Rosa's across the room. She set her lips in a thin line, marched across room and rescued Mr. Wintersmith with a whispered something or other.

"Oh." My mother's voice trilled out loudly enough to be heard by everyone present. "I understand. Go, go. Help the help." She waved Mr. Wintersmith away and turned to assess the company her husband was keeping. Not finding us worthy of her attention, she snapped open her handbag instead, pawed about in its contents and exited the room, presumably to powder her nose.

"That woman didn't *really* give birth to me, did she?" I asked my father in a stage whisper loud enough only to be heard by us at the table. Michael snickered.

My father didn't answer, but he looked at me sharply, his eyes wide. Insult to injury. I was guilty of that.

"Dad, sorry, I'm sorry," I said. "It's just that…" I didn't know what to say. I had never talked with him about how she made me feel, jokingly or otherwise. Now was obviously not the time to start, and making a joke of the issue was not the way to start.

"Excuse me," my father said as he stood up.

"It's just that I don't get her," I said, hurriedly trying to explain myself before he left the table.

"I know, Cass," he said. I felt his hand on my shoulder for the briefest moment, and then he followed my mother's path out of the room.

CHAPTER SIXTEEN

Aiding and Abetting Fate

"Look, Michael, I've got to go to the conference in Santa Cruz. I need to be there," I pleaded into the phone.

"Windler, it's just bad timing…"

"No, make it good timing, make it possible, Michael. You owe me one anyway, I'm sure." I was getting angry. If I went to the conference I could look at the boardwalks, I could check out the area, see why I was having these things, these visions. My hand was sweating. I switched the phone to my left ear and dry hand.

"Cass, you've got two classes and a new grad assistant and it's almost the end of fall semester. Art could still use your help with his Moodle course and there's a production dinner for next year's 'Science at the U' film. It's bad timing."

"Have my grad assistant help Art. Have him teach my classes while he's at it—that's what grad asses are for right?" I was going. Come hell, high water or job termination. I'd already emailed my video contribution to the science update film crew, and I knew my graduate assistant was itching to do more than he'd been given so far. I couldn't handle these visions any longer. I needed to find out whatever the hell I was supposed to know about them. I was going back to the boardwalk.

"Wind…" Michael began.

"Just figure it the fuck out." My voice sharpened. "By the way, you're not even from Mexico and neither are your parents, in case you're wondering if this is another 'Mexican thing.' I'm going." I hung up, tossed the phone onto the table and headed upstairs to start packing.

I could have told Michael why I wanted to go, the real reason, but I'd felt a distance between us since he'd made that "Is this a Mexican thing?" crack. Maybe I was being overly defensive, and if I was, I had better wrap my head around the reason why. But for now, I was telling Michael that I wanted to go to Santa Cruz for purely professional reasons.

As for Asha, she would understand a last-minute conference attendance, I knew. My heart ached to be able to be upfront with her about the reason, but I hadn't told her anything about having seen my future self, scrawny and washed-up and with no trace of her by my side, and I didn't think I should mention anything just yet. I would know more after I visited Santa Cruz. Once I was certain I wasn't losing my mind, I'd tell Asha what was happening.

* * *

As it was, Asha was fine with my going to the conference, as long as we spent some quality time together before my departure. Our sex life had always been on the robust side, both of us enjoying just about every type of sensual adventure we'd ever undertaken, but during the week prior to the conference, we made up in advance for any "quality" time that would be lost during the four days I'd be gone.

"Ash, really, no more," I laughed and tried to push her off me as she wriggled under the covers where I was hiding out, trying to catch my breath from our last tryst.

"Okay." She sat up, creating a tent around us with the blankets and sheet. From this angle with my head on the mattress and hers in the peak of the tent, she looked like a giantess who had wandered into a Bedouin's home. Her breasts looked like little mountains in reverse color, white snow all around capped by wonderfully warm brown earth at the tops.

The giantess leaned down over me, placing her face right in front of mine and whispered, "Okay, but I am going to miss you."

I laughed and pulled her to me in a bear hug. We wrestled around until we were both resting comfortably in each other's arms.

"I'm going to miss you too—ooof!" Out of sight, from above the now-flattened blanket tent we were still in, Wasabi attacked. She'd pounced from god knows where—maybe the dresser—and landed on my abdomen.

"Wasabi!" Asha batted at the blankets from inside our tent, and Wasabi must have batted back because Asha excused herself, left the tent, presumably escorted the cat out of the room, closed the door and returned.

"Are you sure?" she said once she was under the covers again. She eyed the length of my naked body and raised her eyebrows at me in invitation.

"Ash, I haven't run once this week!"

"What's that got to do with…"

"No energy!" I answered. "I've used up all my running energy right here in our bed! And on the living room floor! And in the spare bedroom!"

"Not to mention in the car," Asha added. Unfortunately, taking the walk down short-term memory lane turned me on. We had been rabbits this week. I ran the back of my hand down the front of Asha's body, from her collarbone to her pubic bone. I stopped there, letting the skin on the back of my hand linger over her warmth. She was so soft. What would I do without her, if it ever came to that?

I had to hide a ripple of panic that moved through me as I realized it very well could come to that. What if my trip out to Santa Cruz was the impetus for the life I was seeing in the visions? Should I stay home and avoid becoming the person I had been envisioning for weeks now? Could I control my future by avoiding the place in which I saw my future self? Or was it inevitable?

Asha put her hand in mine, which was still savoring the warmth of her body. Her eyes were soft on mine, and a small smile played on her mouth. She leaned over me and kissed the skin between my eyebrows where I'm sure a deep trough of thought had formed. I couldn't bear the thought of living that life I'd seen without her—maybe I'd skip the trip.

CHAPTER SEVENTEEN

Coasting

I spun Asha's ring around on my finger, wondering if she'd still want to marry me if she knew I was seeing things. Would she want to commit to me if she knew I was going to age into an old weathered crone who worked the Tilt-A-Whirl?

Seeing Santa Cruz and revisiting the boardwalk would help me make sense of the visions. Maybe even help me put them to rest.

That had been the only place I'd ever really felt like part of a normal family. Sticky with ice cream and cotton candy, I'd held my father's neck in the crook of my elbow as we watched the wild adult rides catapult humans into the sky, whip them around and splash them back toward Earth. Behind her huge Jackie O glasses my mother had smiled, albeit with tight lips. The crowds had swollen and shrunk while we walked as a happy, little family unit. I had loved the feeling of it. I remember feeling adequate finally. Not like a charm that my parents were counting on for some magical reason. Not like a bartering tool used by my mother to get attention or pity from my father. Not like a poster child for fertility.

It had been the only family vacation in which we had ever indulged. Memories of it had carried me through the rest of my childhood and into my adolescent years during which I viewed photographs and heard countless wonderful stories about schoolmates' family vacations. They had had, at least, the annual experience of a family holiday to buoy them through fights with their parents, breakups with sweethearts and the banalities of mundane school days. Many of them had even more than one family vacation a year, experiencing travel, beaches, new languages with their brothers, sisters, mothers and fathers, bringing them closer together, giving them memories and a shared history.

In high school, I had all but adopted the Mayer family for two years so that I could experience a semblance of "holiday." With my own parents, I had the one vacation to the Santa Cruz boardwalk, and I clung to it as if it were more precious than air, water and all that is holy.

It was no wonder that I'd wind up there, I guessed, working the seaside rides. But why? Why the change of venues? Why the change in profession? Or lack of profession, if I were honest with myself. Without undoing my airplane seat belt, I leaned over the sleeping woman beside me and tried to see the ground far below us. No luck, we were too high up now, above the clouds, to see anything. The seat belt symbol above me dimmed and the chime dinged, letting us know it was safe to use tray tables and move about the cabin, so I flipped my table down and began writing a postcard, picked up in the Minneapolis-St. Paul Airport, to Asha.

I wrote the words, "Did I ever tell you that my last girlfriend never read the postcards I sent her?" That would be enough for this message. I grinned thinking of Asha smiling as she read it. For a second I felt guilty about not being upfront with her about the real reason I needed to go to the conference in Santa Cruz. The guilt was washed aside as I reminded myself that she'd be marrying some whack-a-doo who had hallucinations if I *didn't* go and try to figure things out.

* * *

Later that night, after checking in, I decided to skip the opening speaker to hang out and dine with some fellow science-geek friends who were also attending the conference. I was itching to get out to the boardwalk to explore the site of my visions, but I had run into Linda Crespo at the conference hotel. It had been so long since we'd seen each other and I had really enjoyed working with her at the U, so I had accepted the dinner invitation. There were five of us: James Huber, a chemistry guru whom I'd never met before, but of whom I'd heard; Linda, who had moved out to California to teach at Berkeley; and Brian Rush and Calvin Armstrong. I'd met Brian and Calvin through Linda at previous conferences, but I hadn't seen them for years. Brian, Calvin and Linda were biologists like me, but surprisingly the talk around the table tonight was about physics—the quantum kind rather than the classical Newtonian action-reaction kind.

"Nothing travels in a straight line anymore," Linda said, tightening her short ponytail.

"Never did," Calvin added. "That's the problem." I had been introducing myself to James when they began this conversation.

"That's what problem?" I butted in. James and I weren't going to be great friends; I could tell this from his reaction when, in response to his question if my husband would be joining us, I told him I had a partner named Asha. For a split second, I saw his nose crinkle up in distaste before he created a more politically correct façade. We had a round table for six, so I took the seat beside Calvin and left an empty space next to James.

"The problem," she began to answer my question, "of why the general public has a hard, if not impossible, time conceiving of twins being able to communicate without spoken words." Upon hearing this, I remembered that Linda had started to get interested in twin phenomena shortly before she had moved out west.

"We all want to believe that we understand communication, that it has to be explicit. Signed…" Calvin used his hands to sign a few words. I thought he signed, "I love my hat," even though he wasn't wearing one. He continued, "Or spoken, or written or smelled. We agree that scents can convey communications of sorts, right?"

"Yes," Linda agreed, "but not many believe that people can communicate across oceans or what have you simply by thinking—or not even that! Some of the people in the study never even tried to communicate with their twin. It just happened!" Linda was excited.

Brian leaned over to me and said, "This is what we've gotten ourselves into recently. Studying twins who are 'telepathy-prone,' as we're calling them. There aren't many who can do it, but..."

"Is it a question of not being capable?" Calvin asked. "Or is it a matter of not thinking oneself capable and therefore not letting oneself *be* capable?"

"Good question," James said, eyeing the waitress up and down as she approached. What a pig jerk, I thought. *How about if you just go away, James?* I caught Linda's eye. She had noticed James's behavior as well.

"At any rate," she sighed, dismissing James, "that is what we aim to discover."

I managed to tell them their research sounded incredible before the waitress took our orders. The time between placing our orders and the arrival of the food was spent with me being regaled by Linda, Calvin and Brian's accounts of twins who telepathically communicated in experimental test situations as well as in self-reported real-life situations. In all cases, the twins who could or had used telepathy had either never been told they couldn't or had been explicitly told they could. In all cases of the twins who could not use any form of telepathy, the twins had all been told that telepathy was a farce, that it wasn't possible for them or others.

"Another thing we'd like to look at in the twins that believe they can't telecommunicate is how they do if they witness other sets of twins, triplets or whatever have success with telecommunication," said Linda. "If they see it, can they do it? It's simple self-efficaciousness building, right? Show them peers doing it, and there you have it! You can do it too. Maybe. Probably." She took a sip of wine and wiped her mouth with gusto. She was pleased with her hypothesis apparently.

Seeing what must have been a look of confusion on my face, Brian restated Linda's enthusiastic idea for me. "Albert Bandura tells us that one way to build self-efficacy for acquiring skills is to show a person that the skill is able to be executed by peers…"

"I get it now," I said. I did get it. It was interesting to contemplate. And it was so far removed from everything I studied at the U, but yet, it was directly related to learning. Without self-efficacy, or the feeling of being able to do something well, in regard to learning, students gave up without even trying to master new knowledge.

"You know," James said drily, "it is more likely that it depends on when the zygote splits into two embryos rather than what people *think* they can do."

"Yeah, we've looked at that theory," Calvin said. "The longer it takes a zygote to split the more identical the twins are. So, yeah, some researchers are looking at the likelihood of these late-splitters being more capable of telepathy, but there's no reliable way to tell when the splitting happened after the fact, is there?"

"I have no idea," James said. "Look it up. It's not that interesting to me, so I never really gave it one thought or another." He sounded peevish. I bet he had wanted to claim that he had just thought of the late-splitter idea himself and was bummed out that they'd heard of it already.

Linda, Calvin and Brian continued to tell me about specific incidences of twin telepathy in their study, and I continued to be amazed. What would it be like to be able to have a conversation with someone who wasn't even in the same city right now? What if I could say something to Asha from here without even picking up my cell phone? Although, it wouldn't be Asha—it would have to be a sibling, a twin. To communicate like that would be unsettling, wouldn't it? Or would it unsettle me just because I thought it should, like they were explaining earlier?

"Oh!" Linda exclaimed, sitting straight up in her chair and pointing at me. "Oh! Your wedding!"

"Yes?" I said. I knew my grin looked like the Cheshire cat's, but I couldn't help it.

"Tell us all about your plans!" Linda demanded. So I did, happily.

James stayed at the bar in the restaurant after dinner. Outside the restaurant, I thanked Calvin, Linda and Brian for a lovely evening. The three of them were heading back to the hotel. Calvin was presenting tomorrow during the conference, so he wanted to get in a good rehearsal. Linda and Brian were going to be his practice audience. I wished him good luck, promised Linda I would keep in touch and ambled toward the boardwalk.

My head was full of twin telepathy theory, details fuzzed and blurred together by the two glasses of wine I'd consumed. I thought about lacing up and jogging past the closed amusement park but decided against it. I'd check out the area tonight, walking, and lace up for an early morning run instead. The lights of the carnival area were darkened, and the roller coasters and Ferris wheel were skeletal creatures in front of the dark blue sky where the sun had set an hour ago. The park wouldn't open until Saturday since it was winter—which here in Santa Cruz was more like early fall in Minneapolis. But I thought I could at least find a bench near the park and see if anything came to me. I didn't necessarily want another vision, but I did want to seek some enlightenment as to what the visions were all about.

The water was relatively calm with only the smallest of crests rolling in onto the beach or pressing the wall that separated the amusement park from the ocean. The very top of each gentle wave still held the light of the sun that had already put itself to bed, but other than those luminous outlines, the water was dark.

If the visions *were* harbingers of a dimmer future than I had originally pictured for myself and not some physical or emotional malady, I wanted to come to terms with the place where that future would be unfolding. My surroundings now didn't seem to be as dreary as the atmosphere of my visions. Things appeared crisper, their colors brighter, but maybe it was because it was after dark. I had to admit, though, that even the taste of the air seemed younger, fresher somehow, than the taste of the air in my visions. Or was I just going crazy? Was this how schizophrenia started? Why was I able to remember how the air tasted in a vision?

I felt my phone vibrate in my pocket. It was a text from Asha asking me to phone her when I could. "Good news," it said. I called her.

"Cassie, hi. How are you? How's the conference?"

"It's okay so far," I answered. "How are you?"

"Guess what?"

"You've rented out my side of the bed to a dog rescue, and you now have eleven sets of mini-dachshund eyes staring at you, and the breeze created by their wagging tails is blowing your hair around like a supermodel's?" I took a shot in the dark.

"Oh my god, you are good," Asha purred, and I heard her smile.

"No, really," I prompted.

"I won the Twin Cities Community Builder Award!"

"Asha, I'm so proud of you! I mean I was proud anyway, but, wow!" My words tumbled all over one another.

"I know, the award ceremony isn't until way after the holidays..." I heard something like ruffling papers on her end of the line. "The invitation says it's not until February twenty-third, but it'll be so cool. And there's this dinner after the award ceremony for my team and me, and you have to come. It's for the volunteer jobs we did in Frogtown." Asha sounded like an excited little kid as she described it to me.

"Congratulations, Ash, you've done a lot for that community; you guys deserve it." Asha's company *had* done a lot for the Frogtown community. They had undertaken much of the volunteer renovation on needy homes, but they had also raised over two hundred thousand dollars for a community center. Asha's company was focused on and licensed for residential property, so the community center had been created by another company, but Asha had been around for a good deal of the work, not to mention the funding.

I put Asha on speakerphone while I recorded the date of the awards dinner in my phone's calendar. She described how excited a few of her employees had been when she shared the news. My heart swelled with pride and happiness for her. At the same time, I felt as if it were physically shrinking with the aching need to tell her what I was really doing this far away from her. *Not just a conference, Asha, but a hunt for reason, for clarity*, I longed to say. But I couldn't. Not if I didn't want her doubting my sanity after she heard what was happening to me. I knew I was being a coward, worrying too much about how Asha would judge me, but this was something I would have to tell her about only after it was no longer a mystery to me. She couldn't know sooner.

The next morning came too early. I wasn't at all interested in going to any of the presentations, but I was here, so I felt I had to attend at least one. The speaker on the stage was temporarily illuminated from behind as the screen lit up with images from her research. The bright edges made me think of the waves from the night before. A thought, unbidden and disconnected from the presenter's words, crashed down upon me like a falling timber. In my evening vision the sunlight had come from *behind* me as I faced the ocean, not from in front of me. There had been no sun setting into the water, only a sunset that lit the buildings from behind—from the *inland* side of the coast. And in the morning vision the ocean had seemed to have just given birth to the sun and its millions of sparkling shards of light.

Was I in the wrong place? On the wrong coast? God damn it. I was. I was in the wrong fucking place. I took my glasses off and looked at them—perspective. I had the wrong perspective here. I mashed shut my eyes and pressed my fingertips hard against my forehead between my brows.

"Are you okay?" a whisper from my right and a hand on my knee wanted to know.

"Yes, thanks," I answered. I put my glasses back on. "Just need a little water," I said before rising, grabbing my satchel and waiting for my concerned neighbor to move her backpack so I could step between her and the backs of the seats in front of her.

"Hot in here," I stage-whispered. She nodded in sympathetic agreement, her eyebrows raising themselves on her forehead like birds about to take flight, and she fanned herself in camaraderie.

She probably thought I was dealing with menopause. She was about twenty-five, so to her I must have looked old enough. At that moment I decided I'd much rather be battling hot flashes than hallucinations and misidentified boardwalks. Hey. Maybe that was it. Maybe the visions were signaling the onset of menopause. I'd look it up once I got to my hotel room.

At least that was my plan. As I watched the elevator doors slide closed before me, I felt a hot tear gloss a path down my cheek. And then another. And one more before I fuck you'd and god damn it'd into my palms and let myself slide to the floor. I was so tired of this! I wanted so badly to be in the right place, figure out why I was having these visions and get on with my life. I didn't want to continue this fruitless chase. The elevator chimed. I snuffled myself into a standing position, gave up on caring how I looked to anyone who might at that moment be catching an elevator from the seventh floor and waited for the doors to slide open. They opened, to my relief, on an empty corridor.

In my room, I threw myself across the bed and let the rest of my frustrations ooze out of my tear ducts. The hotel bed smelled stale and strange and felt foreign against my forehead, so I flipped over to stare at the ceiling while continuing to run my saltwater resources dry.

CHAPTER EIGHTEEN

Art's Confession

"Cassie, I have been meaning to have a discussion with you, but haven't had the guts yet," Art said when I answered his knock at my office door. "I'm experiencing a bit of bravado today after a successful first semester back." It was December twelfth, our last day of instruction for fall semester. Now we only had finals to get through. Art took the chair I offered. I sat down in the remaining chair.

"There's a topic you need guts for—with *me*?" I asked. The surprise on my face may very well have matched the surprise in my voice, and Art reacted by patting my knee. He looked around my office, his eyes landing on the framed Hello Kitty mermaid picture that Asha had colored for me shortly after I'd met her. It was juvenile, and it didn't fit in with the textbooks and reference books that lived in my bookcases, but it made me happy every time I looked at it. The fact that Asha had colored it for me and the fact that she'd colored it with a kid who lived in one of the neighborhoods where she had been doing some volunteer contracting had revealed a lot about her. Art smiled as he looked at it, but too quickly his smile faded, and he turned his focus to me.

"It's okay. Well…" he comforted. "It's not that bad. It could be worse, maybe."

"What is it, Art?" How could he possibly have bad news for me? Was it his health? That would be bad. I hoped he didn't tell me it was his health. I liked this man. I wanted him around for a while. Was he leaving to travel again? What was it? About what could he possibly have to find courage to discuss with *me*?

"The thing is, Cassie, is well, uh, well…" His words stumbled around in his mouth. "I don't know how to…well, let me start at the very beginning."

"Okay," I said, tempted to add the lyric from *The Sound of Music*—"that's a very good place to start."

"I used to be in research, Cassie," Art began. "I dabbled in genetics; I adored recessive gene trait studies, but I also did some work with infertility—I told you, I think, that I did some work with your father?" Art watched my reaction, but apparently there was none, other than my nod of acknowledgment, so he continued.

"I was on a research fellowship at the time, and my whole… my everything depended on my research ethics. I could not afford to mess anything up."

I nodded again. I understood that.

"I also wanted to ensure that my research was as pure as possible because I knew it would affect real people, so it wasn't just the fellowship," he said.

"That makes sense," I said. I had no idea where he was going with this.

"Cassie, I believe your father is a good man," he said. He looked into my eyes as he said it, and I felt my stomach tense. "I believe he started out with the right intentions."

"Art." I had to take a deep breath before I could continue. "I know, well, I know no one is perfect, data sometimes winds up skewed depending on what tests you put it through…I know…" What exactly did I know? I knew I had the feeling that I wouldn't be happy once I heard what Art came to share with me.

"Right, it does sometimes," Art conceded, "but sometimes it is purposefully skewed, and sometimes…other things happen to it."

I listened.

"Cassie, I need to tell you about the research because it leads, I think, to something bigger, something I think you need to be aware of." He broke eye contact, looking at his hands in his lap. His head hung low and a valance of his thick hair tried to curtain his eyes. Art took a deep breath. He sat up straight and pushed his hair back.

"Your father created false data to support the positive impact of a fertility drug. The company paid him over a million dollars to do this." He spoke quickly—so that I didn't have time to react, I think, and stop him from saying what he needed to get off his chest. "I don't think he would have done this except at the urging of your mother, who was his fiancée at the time."

"How do you know this?" I asked. Not challengingly, though. And not because I didn't believe him. I knew with sudden certainty that what he said was true. The ice that formed in my stomach and in my throat upon hearing Art's words corroborated its validity. Even though I had never had any inkling before now that my father might have done something like this, I *knew*. God damn it. I knew my mother's unscrupulous power over him. I also knew of his love for her.

"I was his partner in the project," Art said. He looked up from his hands in his lap. "I knew, and I never told anyone until recently." He sounded so old and tired as he confessed this. "I left the project, made up an excuse, pretended to have a passion about Marshall Nirenberg's cracking of the genetic code—not really a stretch; I really was interested. But I knew I could no longer work on your father's project." His voice dragged through gravel to get out of him. I could hear the air leaving his lungs, making him fragile and vulnerable with his confession.

Silence built itself up like a wall between us, Art now with his eyes glued to my face, waiting, I supposed, for me to say something, and me with my mouth pressed shut so that I didn't scream out all the bitter, angry accusations that my mother deserved. I didn't need to defend her, but I didn't know if I was ready to go where the truth would take me. I didn't want to think of my father's part in this either. What was he thinking when he married her? Was he really who I thought he was—a brilliant man manipulated by a cunning, heartless woman? Or had he been just as much to blame in this?

Thinking of the luxuries I'd had as a child made me feel tainted. I can't honestly say I didn't enjoy the mountains of books, the never-ending parade of new toys, the tiny tree house with indoor plumbing and real windows, but even before hearing Art's story, I'd have traded in all that wealth brought for some genuine affection. Much as I loved those extravagances, it made me nauseous now to know that they had been acquired with money that had come from duping the public. And not just the public, but a particular, rather vulnerable selection of the public—people who were dealing with one of life's injustices, infertility.

I didn't want a wall between Art and me. I looked at his hands, and then I looked at my own. I didn't know what to say. Would he want to hear how I was feeling? How *was* I feeling? I had to say something to keep the wall between us low, because with every second another layer was added to its height.

"My mother would have been much more interested in the money than in research ethics, that is for sure," I said. I felt as if I should have been surprised by this revelation, but I wasn't. I just didn't know where to put this information. Did it belong in my head or in my heart? Did it belong in the public's hands? Where did it belong?

"Art?" I asked. "What am I supposed to do with this?"

"Cassie, my dear," Art said and then he cleared his throat. "There is more."

I said nothing but looked into his eyes to determine just how bad would the rest be.

"There's more," Art repeated. He appeared to be gauging what he saw in my eyes as well. Was he looking to see if I may have already known about this huge secret my parents were concealing? I hadn't, nothing that I'd known for certain anyhow, but could he see that I'd had vague suspicions? I said nothing, but I didn't break his gaze. I had nothing to hide, and I had the feeling I'd need his help with all of this. His bushy eyebrows, one permanently cocked like Peter Falk's, rose and then knitted together as he told me the rest of this news. He patted my hand again, not removing his rough hand from the back of mine until he was done. The whole time he was divulging just how evil my mother was, purging himself of his poisonous knowledge, unbagging the cat and at the same time trying to comfort me, I distanced myself from the situation by wondering how a research professor could come to have such rough hands.

"Cassie," Art sighed, "I apologize for anything that comes of my actions regarding this. I do not mean you any damage. I'm sorry I had to be the one to tell you."

He looked down at our hands, mine clasped in his. He opened his mouth as if to continue speaking, closed it resolutely, but then looked back up at my eyes and continued.

"Cassie, I am so sorry for what is going to happen."

Silence once again followed Art's last words. I couldn't begin to process everything else he'd just shared, much less the bombshell with which he'd concluded. Instead, I looked down at our hands. Whether it was the effects of his travels or the repeated pouring of chemicals from one test tube to another, something had eroded his skin into the dry, sandpapery stuff that enveloped my own—just as my parents' lives were slowly disintegrating before me and blowing off in a thousand different directions.

CHAPTER NINETEEN

Gifts and Carjacking

I wandered, far from alone, the bustling walkways at the Mall of America. With less than two weeks left until Christmas, the shops spilled over with people eager to check off items on their iPhone gift lists, find just the right something for that special someone or drown their holiday misery in gifts bought for themselves.

Each store sported festive trimmings with the single mission of not spreading holiday cheer, but rather enticing patrons to spend, spend, spend and spend some more. The common areas of the mall were decorated with wonderfully oversized adornments. Despite my less than merry mood, the swags of pine, the glittering white lights, the enormous glass balls did indeed make me feel like whipping out my wallet.

I leaned over a banister to watch the line of children on the ground-level floor below waiting to beg gifts from Santa. Bittersweet was the realization that we were conditioned to produce many of our emotions. Bittersweet like the pain in my hipbones against this railing combined with a sweet nostalgia for the days when I believed in a chubby-cheeked man who'd deliver the goods on Christmas morning.

Two little missions and one enormous mission had led me to this behemoth institution. The first two were buying the obligatory gifts for my parents. The other was in no way obligatory. Asha and I weren't big on Christmas gifts for each other—we preferred giving little surprise gifts throughout the year for no apparent reason to the big commercialized gift exchange—but this year I wanted to get her the mother of all gifts, a ring. I looked at my ring. I spun it around on my finger. The center diamond was emerald cut, and it was surrounded by smaller, round diamonds in a platinum art deco setting that had more little diamonds running along the band. It was fussy in a no-nonsense sort of way, delicate yet straightforward. I loved it.

I knew the ring I bought Asha would have to be much more simple, much more clean-lined in its design. I had looked online at styles, and I had narrowed down the field to rings that were not meant for engagement. Those were all too feminine. Asha was feminine acting, but her style was more androgynous. The men's wedding bands were more her style, but I refused to go there and be trapped forever in some June and Ward Cleaver stereotype. She wouldn't want a man's wedding band anyhow. So the ring had to be similar to a man's band, but not really a man's band. I'd look for a wider platinum band with a diamond set into it, something she could wear to work without worrying, yet something that would represent the traditional union. I smiled. Traditional.

For my mother, I was buying a Swarovski crystal angel ornament from Macy's and for my father a gift set of Gucci "Guilty pour homme" cologne from Bloomingdale's. He'd worn the scent for years. Art's words crept back into my head. I knew what he'd said was true, and I probably shouldn't be getting them gifts at all, but I couldn't face it all just now. It was easier to move forward pretending not to know than to… do what exactly? Confront them? Talk to the police? Locate the hundreds of thousands of people who'd been wronged and… right the situation? Impossible.

So instead I shopped. Mother's and Father's gifts were easy. I celebrated with a large quantity of candy bought at an old-fashioned candy shop, which I consumed as I moseyed around the mall in search of Asha's ring.

Finding it proved easier than I had expected, but it didn't happen at the Mall of America. The cookie-cutter designs for wedding-ish rings at the stores there became depressing even before I spied what I believed to be the same exact ring at four different jewelry stores. Were they all secretly owned by the same corporation? I decided I didn't want corporate on my wife's finger.

My wife. Wife. The word jarred me. While the idea of a ceremony to honor and celebrate our love and respect for one another elated me, the word "wife" struck me as subjugating and wrong. Granted, there was power in wielding the word against anyone who thought that what two women could share was less than what could transpire between a man and woman, but the word still jangled around in my head as one that denoted inferiority.

Before I left to find a more personalized, smaller jewelry store in Minneapolis, I realized that I fit into all three categories of MOA shoppers that I had earlier discerned: I had a checklist of gifts, I had shopped for myself and I had attempted to drown out some misery even if that misery was more related to my parents' behavior than to the holidays. I thought, all the while, about the word "wife." If we were both each other's wives, then there could be no imbalance of power, right? There could be no inferiority. Or did a couple of wives automatically imply a lesser union? I put the questions aside and carried on with my mission.

I discovered Asha's ring at a jewelry store named Nicollet Jewelry on, of course, Nicollet Avenue. It was the first store I went to and the first ring I asked to see. I loved its clean simplicity and bold lines, and I could picture it on her finger without imagining hard at all. I hesitated to go with my first choice without first seeing what else was around, however, so I visited four other jewelry shops before coming back to this one.

I examined the ring again once I was in my car. I had to turn the overhead light on since the sun had already sunk beneath the city's tall horizon. It was stunning. I was struck by a painful longing to show the ring to Guadalupe. She would have been so happy for us, not necessarily for the ring itself, but for what it represented. The ring was solid and heavy, made of platinum with a deliciously bright diamond that was set even with the ring's surface, so there were no prongs, which I thought was smart since Asha wasn't the type to appreciate having to unhitch herself from being caught in a sweater or a dishtowel. The diamond was cut into a triangle, which, for a lesbian, was oh-so appropriate.

I was about to slip the ring onto my own finger when there was a firm banging on my window and a muffled hollering outside.

"Christ!" I flinched and the ring went flying into the footwell of the passenger side of the car. I couldn't see the ring, and I was afraid to turn and look at the brute who was no doubt going to carjack me *and* Asha's ring, but I had to look. I squinted my eyes before I turned to see the attacker, as if my eyelids were going to ward off the violence, and between my squinched up lids, I saw Michael's happy face steaming up my window as he waved like a doofus from the cold outside.

"Michael Morales," I bellowed after I opened the window enough for him to hear my pisstivity. "You ass!"

"Sorry, Wind, I didn't mean to scare you," he laughed, making little puffs of steam. "I really didn't."

He ran around the front of the car and waited on the passenger side to be let in. I unlocked the door for him but held him off with the universal "Wait right there, dumbass" hand sign.

"Help me find Asha's ring before you get in," I demanded. "It's on the floor here as a result of your attack on my window."

"Seriously?" he asked.

"Seriously."

We looked around, me from my belted-in position in the driver's seat and Michael from his knees at the curbside. For this

I almost forgave him for his comment weeks ago and for scaring the hell out of me minutes ago. We couldn't find it.

"Hold on," Michael said. He took off his glove and rummaged around under the seat.

"I got it!" He held Asha's ring up between us. He whistled and nodded, inspecting the ring.

"Nice, hey?" I asked.

"Seriously nice." He was still nodding. He ducked into the passenger seat, made himself comfortable and handed me the ring. "I'd wear it, that's for sure," he said.

"Well, if things don't work out with Asha…" I let my voice trail off.

"Does that mean you're not mad at me anymore?"

"I should be even madder after the car attack."

"Yeah, my bad. Didn't mean to scare you," he chuckled.

"What're you doing here?" I asked. He had on a nice woolen coat over what appeared to be an equally nice suit.

"Date."

"Date?"

"Yup."

"Is that all you're going to tell me?" Michael was not usually a one-word answer kind of guy.

"I'm afraid I'll jinx it, you know? If I tell you how much I enjoyed her company. It was a lunch date, and we just now said goodbye."

"Wow, long lunch," I mused. He hadn't dated much at all since he and Holly had divorced. Or if he did date, he didn't mention it.

He smiled at me and nodded yet again.

"Well, I don't want you to jinx anything," I said, "but…okay, good!" I couldn't wish him well with this long lunch gal because that too might jinx things.

"Thanks," he said.

I tucked Asha's ring back into its little velvet box before another carjacker came by and made me toss it into one more dark corner of the car. "I wonder how many other superstitious scientists there are out there."

"Humph," Michael snorted, "all scientists are superstitious, I bet. It's the only mystery we have left in this world. Well, that and girls."

"Yeah," I laughed with him. "We've always got girls."

CHAPTER TWENTY

Merry Christmas

The scents of cinnamon, coffee and pine greeted us as I entered my parents' dark mahogany front door. It was Sunday night, December twenty-third, and my parents had invited us over for a holiday dinner before they embarked on a cruise. It was an unusual invitation that had us both on edge. I knew Asha couldn't really feel it through her thick woolen peacoat, but I kept my hand at the small of her back until we were inside to lend her support in what I believed was going to be an abusive tumble down a rocky, albeit Christmas-scented, cliff.

"Did I ever tell you my last girlfriend never fed me to the wolves?" Asha's black eyes sparkled as she teased me.

I knew she saw possible adventure in this dinner at my parents' house, but it never ceased to awe me how she continued to turn blatant disrespect from my mother into a funny anecdote to be mused over later. Neither of us had experienced the family life we had wanted to as children, yet we both kept coming back, still seeking.

I had not spoken to Asha about the topics Art had shared with me. I was still coming to terms with them myself. I thought I might be able to suss out some truth tonight in what he had said, even though in the deepest recesses of myself, I knew he had spoken fairly and honestly of my corrupt parents.

I now was keeping two secrets from Asha—secrets that were too big to not share, I knew—and that was eating at me. Perhaps deception ran in my veins. Could it be hereditary? Had I told Asha what Art had shared, though, I'd end up spending the whole night trying to figure out what she was making of my parents and their actions in light of what she saw before her now...and frankly, I needed to do that for myself before I could wonder about her perceptions.

I took Asha's coat from her shoulders, thin and angular in their black velvet jacket, and murmured, "Yes, and that's why you had to leave her—she let the wolves starve to death. You let her know she was history right after you called the ASPCA."

We didn't have time to acknowledge our joke because my father, who must have heard the front door close, appeared in the foyer to help us with our coats and packages. He looked dapper, as usual, in a midnight blue three-piece suit with a resplendent emerald shirt and darker tie and pocket square. His smile reached his eyes, and he warmly hugged both of us.

"Glad you're here, girls," he said as he swept open the closet door, deposited our coats on hangers and pressed the door closed—the whole operation silent as a librarian shelving books. There were never any echoes in my parents' house because very rarely were any noises allowed to occur. It was as if the thick rugs, paintings and rich wallpapers absorbed every sound wave. Asha picked up the insulated warming bag that contained the whipped sweet potatoes and a canister of our homemade five-spice peanuts, Asha's favorite shout-out to her Asian heritage. She waited for me to grab the two small gift bags from Macy's, and then all three of us took deep breaths and flung ourselves over the craggy edge into the abyss that was my mother.

We had not had many Christmas dinners as a family as I was growing up. More often than not, when I was young, it was Guadalupe and I who celebrated together while my parents attended conferences in warmer climates. Thinking back, I wonder how many conferences there really could have been—wouldn't most other doctors and their spouses be sharing the holidays with their families?

In these past few years, Asha and I'd make Christmas dates with Guadalupe, and we'd meet at her apartment for decadent romeritos and bunuelos, as well as lively music and raucous laughter. She'd tell us who she saw at midnight mass the night before, what they were wearing and what they were doing to celebrate today. Guadalupe had a sharp memory for fashion, and she loved describing the fabrics and the colors that comprised her friends' best holiday wear. Even though I could still feel her in my heart, I was saddened to be walking into this house knowing she'd never be here with me again.

My mother glided into the front hall to greet us with cold kisses and hugs that aborted the moment her fingertips touched our shoulders.

"Merry Christmas, Cassie, Asha," she sang. She eyed Asha up and down, no doubt disapproving of her pants suit.

"Merry Christmas," we both chimed. I bit my lip after hearing how hopeful we sounded.

"Come in and see the tree!" my mother said. She clapped her hands together under her chin as if she didn't know what else to do with them, spun toward the dining room and sailed toward the distraction the tree would provide.

"Ohhhh, it's beautiful," Asha murmured when she rounded the corner into the dining room.

"It was decorated by hired help," my mother said, "who probably don't even have Christmas trees themselves!" She tittered behind one delicate, manicured pale hand. "Poor things!"

"We gave them a huge tip, though, so maybe..." my father added. Asha looked at me and I couldn't meet her eyes. Christ. Was this woman really related to me?

"The tree is wonderful, Mother," I said. "The people who decorated it had nice taste."

"Well, that was really me, wasn't it? I mean, I had to search online for the ornaments—oh!" My mother spotted the gift bags I still held.

"We brought you gifts," I said and held them out to her.

"Oh, you shouldn't have! But I am so glad you did!" Her voice was too loud for just the four of us, even in this huge room. No sooner had it sliced through my head, however, than the lavish décor gobbled it up, leaving me with just a piercing echo ringing in my ears. She grabbed the gift bags and headed over to sit in the dining room's bay window. She threw herself onto the settee like a greedy child hopping onto Santa's lap. Her perfect hair didn't even swing with this motion. Her flawless skin, no doubt pampered at some spa that morning, glowed in the carefully crafted lighting. Was she plastic? I really didn't like her.

"Come sit, Lawrence, I'll open both of them," she called to my father.

Asha and I followed her. I motioned for Asha to sit in the dark red velvet chair beside the settee, and I scooted a dining chair off the thick rug and onto the hardwood floor, closer to the little group.

"Watch the floor, Cassie darling," my mother said. I tried to pick the chair up to move it, but it was too heavy to go far with it like that, so I wound up sitting a little further away from Asha than I would have liked to.

"First, let me pour us all a champagne," my father said. He was already at the bucket of ice that stood, chilling the bottle, beside the sideboard. Four champagne flutes had been lined up on their silver tray like little soldiers awaiting commands. There was an awkward moment devoid of conversation as my father wrestled the cork from the bottle. The pop and fizz of success made the crystal soldiers necessary.

"Yeaaaa…." Asha was the only one who cheered the uncorking. Her voice dwindled out by itself. I smiled at her but couldn't bring myself to cheer with her. My father paraded each filled flute over to its new commander.

Finally, he sat down beside my mother. He made a point of smiling at both Asha and me as he raised his glass toward the middle of our small group. Asha and I did the same and sipped our champagne with my father. My mother, however, had set her glass on the windowsill behind the settee without tasting it or toasting the night. She sifted the Swarovski angel out of the gift bag that was meant for her.

"Positively charming, darling," she cooed. The emptiness of her voice echoed in my heart. "Thank you." She held the angel up for my father to see.

"Ah, lovely." He nodded at my mother and then at me. He smiled, and the corners of his eyes crinkled. He looked again at the angel held aloft. It was illuminated by the warmth of the Christmas tree lights and the chandelier's glow. It was beautiful. And it was quickly given a place on my mother's lap as she dug into the gift bag meant for my father. I downed the rest of my champagne, appearances be damned. I needed to buffer myself tonight. I stood to put my empty glass on the dining room table and returned to my chair. Asha's new ring sparkled on her hand as she sipped at her champagne. Poor thing didn't know what she was marrying into, and my heart ached with that knowledge. I decided I would tell her everything—about both the visions and my parents' corruption—later that night after we got home.

"Well, Lawrence," my mother said, "this must be for you!" She passed the bottle of "Guilty" to my father, and he slit the plastic wrap with his thumbnail and flipped open the top of the box.

"Huh," he chuckled, "how did you know I'd just run out?"

"It's true, he did," my mother chimed. A few seconds after he shot fine mist toward his collar and neck, my father's signature scent and the onset of a champagne buzz comforted me.

"That's the way gifts are supposed to work," Asha said. "Just when you need it, there it is!" Her black eyes sparkled. I smiled at her, and so did my father.

"Thanks, girls," he said and leaned over to pat Asha's knee. My chair was further out of reach, so he handed the bottle to my mother, and he stood up to stoop over me. He kissed the top of my head. "Thanks, Cass," he said.

The peal of the doorbell ended the ordeal of the gift giving. My parents hadn't offered gifts to Asha and me, which was fine by me, but I felt that they might be feeling awkward for not having thought of it.

"I'm already up," my father said. "I've got it." He went to answer the door.

"Well!" my mother sputtered. "It's odd timing, isn't it? For someone to call on us?"

"Mmm..." I said. I was listening to the hushed voices in the foyer. My muscles had tensed because the conversation was so soft. I had expected a jovial "How are you? Good to see you!" type of greeting, and the quiet dialogue felt ominous. I looked from my mother, to Asha and back to my mother. It was bad news at the door; I just knew it. But what bad news?

Oh. Could it be, already, the issue Art had divulged? No, it couldn't be, not yet. Not like this.

"Margaret," my father said quietly as he walked into the room with two men in long dark coats trailing him. "Girls, why don't you go wait in the family room downstairs," my father suggested. I ignored him, but Asha stood and took a step toward the dining room table. When I didn't stand up, Asha came over to stand behind my chair. The two men seemed to be waiting for me to do something, but I couldn't move.

"Mrs. Windler," the younger of the two began, "I'm Agent Daniels with the Federal Bureau of Investigation, and this," he motioned to the older man standing to my father's left, "is Agent McCorvey. We need to speak with you about your Parents of Differently Oriented Children charity." He didn't offer his hand for shaking but rather stood there with his hands clasped in front of his groin as if he knew how my mother was about to react.

My mother stood up sharply, dropping the gifts that had been resting in her lap. The shattering of crystal and glass caused a distraction but was no competition for my mother's knifing voice. She grated out her words, "Not without my attorney."

I wanted to stand, but I didn't trust my legs to hold me. Asha stayed behind me, gripping the back of the chair I sat on. On the floor, shards of bottle and angel lay like fractured diamonds in an expanding pool of cologne, which was enveloping us in the scent of Gucci's "Guilty." The irony was not lost on me.

"Well, then, ma'am, sir, you are both under arrest for fraudulent charity activity, corrupt activity, money laundering and crimes related to these charges," Agent Daniels said quietly.

No, not like this. Art you should have warned me better—not like this, not now. My head began to ache.

He took a card from the breast pocket of his shirt and began reading, "You have the right to remain silent. Anything you say will be used against you in a court of law. You have the right to an attorney. If you cannot afford an attorney…" here he looked around him and then at his partner Agent McCorvey before continuing, "one will be provided for you. Do you understand these rights I have just read to you?"

The question hung in the air. I noticed, for the first time, that a Christmas carol was playing over the surround sound. "Silent Night" filled the void until Agent McCorvey prompted, "Do you understand these rights, ma'am?"

"Yes," my mother spat.

"Sir," McCorvey looked at my father, "do you understand these rights?"

"Yes, sir, I do," my father said. His olive skin was so pale. His eyes were wide. They glistened in the chandelier's soft light. He looked at me then and said, "Cassie. Cassie, I am so sorry."

"Do not say a word, Lawrence." My mother ground out her words. "Not one word."

"Please turn around. I am going to place handcuffs on you, ma'am. It's procedure," Agent Daniels said.

I braced myself for the almighty fit she'd throw, but she surprised me by turning around and holding her wrists together behind her. My father did the same. That's when it finally struck me that this was real, this was happening. This was no movie.

A ragged sob cut through the quiet. The sound startled me, but it had come from my chest, my throat, my mouth. In an instant, Asha had her arm around me, pressing me to her side. My shoulders heaved as I attempted to control my crying. Tears spilled, but I managed to lower the volume. Charity fraud. My father. He knew, he *knew*!

Art had not mentioned him when he told me of his suspicions regarding my mother's charity. It wasn't just the fertility drug data my father had skewed; it was bigger than that. Charity fraud? How could he be involved as well? It wasn't just my mother? How could I have not known?

"Cassie," my father pleaded, but I couldn't look him in the eye. I heard guilt in his voice. My mother still said nothing.

"Dr. Windler, Mrs. Windler, let's go now," Agent McCorvey said. To me he said, "We're taking them to FBI headquarters in Brooklyn Center. Here's the number you can call."

He handed me a white business card and then put his hand on my father's shoulder. He kept it there as my father followed my mother and Agent Daniels toward the front door, toward the holiday chill outside.

I stood, finally, on shaking legs. As I trailed behind them, I noticed the oddest things. Like the cream-colored satin wallpaper in the hall to the foyer, which had bars on it, long bars of lighter cream surrounded by long bars of darker cream containing tiny flecks of glittery copper. And the way my father's shadow darkened bar after bar, intermittently turning off the glitter and then letting it come back on as he passed.

My father looked back at me one last time as he was crossing the threshold. I looked him squarely in the eye in return and tried to convey some peace, some understanding—even though I had absolutely none of either.

I sagged against the open front door frame and watched as the agents guided my parents into either side of a black Lincoln parked at the top of the drive's turnaround in front of the house. Lazy, fat snowflakes swirled in the air. The car's windows were tinted, and for a fleeting moment, I had the sensation they were being kidnapped, perhaps to be held for ransom. I let the idea go as quickly as it came, knowing it was just another false security fantasy I'd concocted. They were in trouble that they had created for themselves.

"Oh my god," Asha murmured behind me. "Cass?" I couldn't answer. I couldn't say anything. I just watched the long black car move forward down the driveway and out onto the road. I wrapped my arms around myself, not because I felt the bite of the air, but because I felt alone. Even with Asha right beside me, I was painfully aware of my lack of family. Lupe was gone, and, for the time being, so were my parents.

That night Asha held me so tightly in bed. There was no lovemaking, no talk, no crying; she just held me. We had asked my parents' two housekeepers to help themselves to the lavish dinner that they had prepared for the four of us. They did not seem surprised at what had happened, and neither did they seem upset by it. I can't imagine they saw my parents as anything more than employers, despite the fact that both of them had lived in the house with my parents for over ten years. I wondered if they would be subjected to the FBI's questioning. I was certain I would be. I knew I should talk to Asha before that happened, but now I was too emotionally tired to do anything other than be held.

CHAPTER TWENTY-ONE

The Gun

"Wake up, Cass." My shoulder was being jostled. "Wake up, baby."

"What...?" I managed to murmur, "what?"

"You're having a bad dream," Asha said. Her voice held quiet concern.

"Yeah, I think I was." I rolled over and burrowed my face into a cooler nest of pillows. My chest felt tight. I tried to take a deep breath, but the bedsheets and my own tension thwarted me. I rolled onto my back and stretched out, making myself as long as possible. My skin was damp and cold. I shivered until I'd shoved and kicked the sweat-soaked bedclothes away from Asha and myself. I pulled up the down comforter. That was still dry.

"You okay?"

"No," I answered.

"What was it? You were whimpering, kind of, and you jerked—hard."

"I dreamt I found a gun, in a nightstand," I said. "And I had this really...bad feeling about it."

"Why?" Asha's fingertips found my bare hip. She spread her hand over my belly, and the heat of her skin comforted me. She moved closer to me so that she could ease her arm across my body and pull me nearer to her. In the dream, I'd watched my hand, tan and dry-skinned, reach out toward the drawer on the nightstand. My hand had been tentative—as if I'd known I wouldn't be happy with what I'd find in the drawer.

"Why'd I dream it? Or why did I have a bad feeling?" I asked.

"Well, yeah, now both." Asha's face was against the side of my head, and her voice was even quieter. I thought she might fall back into sleep before I'd sorted out the answer to either question.

"I don't know," I said anyway. "I think the gun was going to be used against me, later on."

Once I'd opened the drawer and had seen the gun, I'd pulled my hand back to the base of my neck as if the weapon were going to burn or bite me. My knuckles had rapped against my collarbone. I'd sounded hollow. I had peered closely at the gun then. The words "Colt .380 Mustang Pocketlite" were engraved into the barrel. It hadn't been a huge gun, but I'd no real experience with guns, so I hadn't thought about the size for long. The cold, unforgiving metal sheen of the hateful thing had left its impression on me, though.

"Later in your dream?" Asha asked. She was still awake.

"Yeah."

"I'm glad you are out of that dream, then," she said and kissed me above my ear. She left her lips there, and I enjoyed the feel of her breath in my hair and on my cheek. "You're all wet," she said, but she kissed me again.

"I know, sorry," I said.

She ran her tongue over the top curve of my ear, and I began to forget about the gun.

"And you're salty," she murmured. I felt a heat begin to kindle deep in my core.

"Probably," I whispered. She tugged at my ear with her teeth like a puppy who can't decide if she wants to wake her littermates to play or roll over and slumber on.

"Would you like a distraction?" she asked as she began stroking my belly with more insistence. I took no time in contemplating my answer.

"Yes, please." And Asha took no time in delivering her offered diversion.

* * *

An hour or so later, Asha lay snore-purring in my arms. There were no covers left on the bed, cold-sweat-soaked, hot-sweat-soaked or any other. We'd done our best to dislodge the dream gun from my mind, but unfortunately, after all had been said and done, I had remembered what had happened earlier with my parents and the FBI.

I'd had to choke back a sob when my memory of the evening's debacle had clawed back through my memory, scratching so closely at the heels of a wonderful orgasm, Asha had assumed, I believe, that my guttural cry was related to our bed activities. That had unleashed a few of her own cries and completion, so I didn't ruin her fun or our connection by revealing to her the true source of my sob. The afterglow had then flowed backward from my extremities, to my limbs, to my torso, fizzling out right where it had begun. I replayed the arrest over and over, my heart growing more and more scared and cold, until Asha slept in my arms. I thought I might go crazy. The prickles of another cold sweat threatened.

I turned my head slightly to rest my cheek against Asha's forehead. How could I worry when I was here, safe, in her arms? I took deep breaths that matched Asha's. I tried to will myself to sleep. She was so warm and pliant against me...

My parents were in serious trouble. I saw my father's hand snake into the nightstand drawer to pull out the gun, the frightening metallic weapon glinting in the Christmas tree lights like another decoration. My father pointed the gun at Agent McCorvey...

I started, fully awake again, and Asha sighed in her sleep. She nestled in closer to me, so I wrapped my arm more tightly about her back and shoulders. She sighed again, still sleeping. The need to talk this through with her ate away at me. I needed to hear, from her, that she wouldn't leave me because of my parents' crimes. I also needed to hear her tell me she wouldn't leave me just because I was having visions of myself, older and alone, without her by my side.

I was in too deep. I hadn't given her a chance to react to my visions, let alone tell me she'd not leave me because of them. I hadn't shared one word about them, and now, with my parents' arrests on top of the vision issue… It was one thing to let your sweetheart comfort you about some random nightmare, but to bare your soul about visions and family crimes…wasn't that quite another thing?

I lay there, astounded that I was even having to contemplate charity fraud. What had gone so wrong? How could I not have known? Had Guadalupe known? Wouldn't she have told me? She had told me everything. She used to hold me so tightly after bad dreams. Like this, like Asha. Differently, but with her arms just as tight.

Random nightmares. God damn them. My breath, raspy and short once again, caught in my throat. Had this been a random nightmare? Had it been? Hadn't it been more realistic, like my visions? Hadn't I recognized the dry, tan skin of my vision-self's forearm and hand? Hadn't I known that bed, that nightstand?

No. I exhaled as slowly as I could. I had not seen the bedroom, the gun, the…anything anywhere before. It had been a dream, that's all. It was only the hour of the night that had made it all seem surreal.

No, not surreal. Real. It had seemed *real*. Hot tears filled the confines of my wide-open eyelids. I turned my head slightly away from Asha's so that my jagged breathing wouldn't wake her, and the tears flowed. I had no choice but to let them. They created rivulets running back through my hair and into the pillow, but at least they wouldn't drip onto Asha, this lovely, sweet woman who deserved so much better than I was giving her with all these crazy worries and dramas.

I lay there knowing I needed to tell her what was going on. Maybe tomorrow or later today, really. What time was it anyway? Yes, I would tell her.

Feeling better after making that decision, I drifted near sleep. At some point, the gun dream replayed itself for me. I watched myself in the familiar, yet unfamiliar bedroom as I looked over my shoulder, carefully pushed the drawer closed and turned out the light.

CHAPTER TWENTY-TWO

And a Happy New Year?

"I've always had a thing for Asian women," a subtly beautiful woman was saying to Asha in a not-so-subtle manner. "Probably started with my lust for anime." The woman, Beth, was a tax attorney that Asha's company had used this year for the first time. She leaned in toward Asha, and I saw her breast graze Asha's arm. It looked like she was either going to kiss her or tell her something in confidence. What the hell? Asha's face showed surprise, and she leaned away from Beth. My neck was going to break from the angle I was contorted into in order to see this whole affair.

"I…uh, excuse me," Asha said. She took a few paces away from the woman, looked around and spied me spying on her. She smiled at me and came over to join the small group of women I had been chatting with.

"Did you hear that?" she whispered to me. She grabbed my bent elbow, and I had to steady myself so I didn't spill my wine from the jostling of my arm. I nodded and suppressed a smile.

"So, if we can get them to give reasons for their irresponsibility…Cassie?" Rebecca Reese was trying to keep my attention on her dilemma with her undergrad students. I was being a shitty hostess.

"Sorry, Bec," I offered, pulling my attention back to the conversation. I switched my wineglass to my other hand, and I grabbed Asha's hand to keep her there by my side. "I'm sorry."

"So, right, my plan is to ask them what their plan is, you know?" I nodded, and Rebecca carried on describing the assignment that was going to bring out the best in her students. What was Beth thinking? Did she seriously not know Asha and I were together? I wasn't feeling very festive anyway after having to talk to the FBI yesterday and visiting my father while he was in their custody this morning, so this woman rather blatantly hitting on Asha was adding insult to injury. Asha must have sensed this because she stroked my inner wrist with her thumb as she held my hand.

"Wind!" a big voice boomed across the room. It was Michael, I knew before turning around. When I did turn to greet him, I was caught off guard by how handsome and happy he looked. He glowed. His black curls had been recently cut shorter, and the look really suited him. His cheeks were rosy from the cold outside, and on his arm rested the hand of a beautiful woman. She smiled at me, her eyes shy, from across the room as Michael pointed me out to her. I raised my wineglass to them and smiled back.

A few minutes later, Michael had taken care of their coats, had secured drinks for them and had joined our group. He patiently waited for an opening in Rebecca's monologue.

"Cassie Windler," he said as soon as Rebecca noticed she was monopolizing the conversation, "I'd like you to meet Melinda Sutton. Mel, this is Windler, my favorite professor friend and running buddy." I let go of Asha's hand to shake Melinda's hand.

"Nice to meet you, Melinda."

"You too," she said. She had chin-length brown hair that had strands of silver in it. Her face was fine-boned with big brown eyes and a cupid-bow mouth. She had a pretty little pixie's face. She smiled at me, and I liked her immediately.

"This is my fiancée Asha," I said, including her in the introduction.

"Hi, it's nice to meet you," Asha said. They didn't shake hands, but they grinned at each other.

"You too," Melinda repeated herself. "Your home is wonderful; it feels good to be here," she said. "I love the woodwork and the colors."

"Asha renovated it," I said proudly.

"Thanks," Asha said, looking around at her own handiwork. As she peered about the room, I did the same, only instead of admiring our home, I took stock of who had arrived and who had yet to show up. Sunny and Anna were cozied up to one another on one side of the couch. Jenn was perched on the arm of the same couch. My eyes stopped there because Jenn was glaring across the room at something. It was such an unusual countenance for Jenn that I followed her gaze to see what she was looking at. I was surprised to find myself making eye contact with Beth. She was staring back at me, and even though I was now gawking at her, she didn't break her gaze. I glanced away quickly. Ugh. I didn't have a good feeling about that one.

I avoided looking in Beth's direction as I continued to tally up the guests. Whitney and Cory were talking to a man and a woman who worked for Asha's company, and there was a group of two of my colleagues and three more of Asha's builders chatting with each other, laughing, in the middle of the living room. Only Esme was missing. She had let me know she was overbooked but that she'd try to get here before we ushered in the New Year.

Since almost everyone was here, I decided it was time to dance. I excused myself from the group I had been talking to, dimmed the living room lights, turned on the rotating disco ball Asha had suspended from the ceiling for the evening, flicked on the two spotlights that were aimed at the disco ball and hit play on my iPod. The group who'd been chatting in the middle of the living room now found themselves in the middle of a dance floor.

"At first I was afraid"—our surround system set the stage for them—"I was petrified." One woman left the dance floor, but two more joined the group that stayed. "Kept thinking I could never live without you by my side," Gloria Gaynor sang out from the speakers. The group in the middle of the room was only swaying minimally to the slow start of the song. But by the time Ms. Gaynor belted out, "But now you're back from outer space," Michael pranced Melinda and Asha out to the dance floor, and the living room was transformed into a proper discothèque complete with flailing aims, gyrating hips and whooping theatrics.

"Always a crowd-pleaser," Beth suddenly purred next to me as I smiled at the dancing mass. I looked at her, even though I'd rather have ignored the comment and walked away. She looked me up and down so seductively that I wasn't sure if she had been referring to me or to the song. That letch, James, from the Santa Cruz conference popped into my mind.

"It is a good song," I said noncommittally and walked away. I headed into the dining room to see what dishes might need replenishing. The hummus and pita chips were both running low, as was the cheese tray, so I headed into the kitchen to get more of each. Beth followed me. I decided to be as kind as possible. She was probably just a big flirt like Jenn, and once I got to know her better, I'd likely find her amusing rather than threatening and annoying. Even so, I couldn't think of a thing to say to her. I busied myself with topping off the low plates and bowls.

"So, have you and Asha lived here long?" she asked.

"Yeah, a pretty long time," I answered, again, noncommittal. I didn't feel like giving her a number of years. I'd decide what was a long time in this case, thank you very much.

"That's cool," she said.

"How about you?" I asked. I knew she could take my question in a number of ways—have you been with your person long? Where do you live? Have you lived there long? Do you have a person?

"How about me what?" she countered. *Damn it.*

"Where do you live? How long have you been there?"

"I have a place in Uptown, been there a little while," she answered. Wow. She out-noncommittaled me.

"Cool."

"So," she began, waiting until I looked at her to carry on, "what's it like being with Asha?"

Seriously? "Seriously?"

"Yeah, what's she like?" I didn't say anything. All I could do was stare at her. I felt my eyebrows furrowed together and my upper lip kind of curl up. I swallowed and tried to smooth my face's reaction to her question. What the fuck was wrong with this woman?

Since I didn't respond, she elaborated, "You know, sometimes you know someone, and you just wonder...you just want to know what it would be like to know her better." Her eyes bore into mine. She waited for me to answer. I wondered if she was being like this on purpose or if she was just clueless. Since she was an attorney, there was no way in hell I was giving her the benefit of the doubt. She was doing this on purpose.

"Beth, right?" I asked. She nodded. I stopped refilling the pita chips, set the bag down on the counter and faced her square on. "Well, Beth, I have bad news for you. You, unfortunately, will just have to keep wondering what it's like to be with Asha because *you* will *never* get to find out for yourself."

She smiled at me, and I grabbed the bowl and started to walk out of the kitchen with it.

"It's fun to see someone who thinks she knows what's going on in her relationship," she laughed. She breezed past me, exiting the kitchen before I could. I took the bowl back to the countertop, set it down and pressed my fingertips between my eyebrows. Christ. What the hell was that about?

Jenn and Asha came laughing into the kitchen. Asha patted my butt on her way past me to retrieve two bottles of wine from the rack.

"S'up, buttercup?" Jenn asked me playfully. Asha wrestled the cork from one of the bottles.

"Having fun?" she asked me.

"Not so much," I answered. "That Beth woman is a bit much."

"Ugh, she's terrible!" Jenn exclaimed. "Do you know," she lowered her voice to finish her question, "I have a feeling she's Esme's Elizabeth."

"Nooo, she can't be," Asha said, giving up on the second bottle and handing it to me. The cork had broken half off. I pushed the half that remained into the bottle with my pinky finger. Asha continued, "She's been carrying on with some woman in Stillwater, but holding out for another woman in St. Paul…oh." Asha's face fell. "Oh no."

"Ah, *yeah*," Jenn said. "That pretty much confirms it. And to think you all wanted to crown *me* Player of the Year!" Asha looked at me as if she wanted to say something, but she said nothing. I couldn't read her expression. "Home" by Edward Sharpe and the Magnetic Zeros started blasting out in the living room disco. That was one of our favorite songs to dance to. I decided to stop worrying about things and enjoy myself, and Asha must have decided the same because she grabbed my hand, pulled me out of the kitchen and onto the dance floor, and we started dancing and bouncing around like idiots. It seemed that everyone knew the lyrics. We were all singing loudly, badly and happily, and Asha was smiling deep into my eyes as she sang, "Home is wherever I'm with you, ohhhh home!" I thoroughly enjoyed dancing with my fiancée for the next half hour, and the worries and pisstivity regarding Beth were erased. Even my worries about my parents were temporarily allayed.

Asha and I found ourselves in a crumpled, hot pile in the corner of the couch by the time someone called out that it was eleven thirty. The night had flown by. There was a vibration on my thigh, and Asha pushed her hips up to wrest the cell phone from her pocket. She read the incoming text.

"Cass, baby?" Asha asked as she sat up beside me. She held my hand.

"Yeah?"

"I've got to go do something, okay? But I'll be right back." She stood up and let my hand fall to the empty couch cushion next to me. Anna quickly filled the space with herself.

"Oh my god!" she exclaimed, sounding kind of buzzed. "This is a good party! Thank you!" She clapped her hand onto my knee and gave me a shake. I smiled at her. Her hair was plastered to her forehead from working so hard on the dance floor. She looked so happy. Sunny threw herself across my and Anna's laps and lay there on her back, laughing and panting.

"Good party," she said, and she patted my cheek. She was drunk. I laughed down at her beaming face.

"It is a good party, you're right," I agreed with her. I could just make out Asha and Beth standing in the foyer near the front door. Asha was shaking her head and talking hard. Beth was holding her coat in front of herself, draped over one bent arm. She was smiling coyly. I tipped my head a bit to the left to see more of them, but then the dancers occluded the view. Damn it. I looked down at Sunny's still-smiling face. Her eyes were closed. I looked back up to Asha and Beth. Asha reached out to Beth, took her coat from her arm, unfurled it and held it out for Beth to step into. Oh thank goodness, my heart had almost stopped there for a second. Beth turned, now ready to leave, and cut a glance at me all the way across the room. She smiled icily. Asha didn't turn to look at me but placed her hand on Beth's lower back to guide her out the door. *Do not follow her out, Asha, do not follow her.*

She didn't follow her out. Instead she closed the door behind Beth and made her way through the revelers to the kitchen. She was in there for a few minutes before she reemerged with two fresh wineglasses filled with water. She met my eyes as she made her way over to the couch.

"What, I'm gone for five minutes, and I've been replaced?" she asked.

"Yes," Anna replied, "and not just by one woman, but by two! Better be careful, Asha." I looked sharply at Anna, and she was smiling at Asha.

Asha grinned back and handed me a glass of water. She got comfortable on the wide arm of the couch and wrapped herself around my shoulders. She kissed me on the top of my head. I leaned my head back into her for a kiss on the mouth. She kissed me, her tongue lazily grazing my lower lip, and then rubbed her cheek against mine.

"Esme's on her way," she said.

"What?" I asked. I didn't make the transition from her mouth to the topic of Esme very smoothly.

"Esme. She texted me to let us know she's on her way," Asha explained. "I thought I should get rid of Beth—Jenn was right, she is Esme's Elizabeth."

"Oh," I said. "Ohh, yeah, that would have been horrible."

"Yeah," Asha agreed. "I'm sorry I invited her—I had no idea."

"She is kind of…" How could I describe her? "She's kind of intense."

"Yeah," Asha agreed. "You can say that again!"

CHAPTER TWENTY-THREE

The Letter

On the morning of February twenty-second, after nearly two exhausting months of visits with my father, meetings with his attorney, soul-searching with myself and going crazy over these visions I was still having, I awoke with the oddest sensation of having been wrapped tightly and warmly—and rather wetly—in some sort of water cocoon. In my half dream, I had been rocked and held, rocked and held, rocked and held by a great, gentle force. I had been moving my mouth and waving both hands, balled into fists, and I felt nothing and I felt everything at the same time. I had no thoughts, really, just sensations—including the pull of the being who was sharing the space with me. She was also being rocked and held, rocked and held. She was connected to me. I gasped like a fish out of water and opened my eyes in the dark. When I was finally, fully awake I realized I had been nuzzling my face against the back of Asha's shoulder.

I got out of bed, both bothered and comforted by the dream, threw on some yoga pants and a hoodie and went downstairs. I paused in front of the big living room window and peered outside before deciding to take care of at least a few of the items on a long and long neglected to-do list. The moon was fat, nearly full and breathtakingly bright. The sight of it held me hostage for a few moments. When I was able to tear my eyes away from it, I headed down to the frigid, damp basement to bring up the laundry I had left spinning in the dryer the night before.

I flipped the switch at the top of the staircase, and the narrow passage lit up. The basement stairs creaked as I descended into the chill. As soon as my feet left the painted wood of the steps and met the clammy cold of the cement, I wished I had put on socks before coming down here. At the bottom of the stairs, I flipped the switch for the two bare bulbs hanging in the largest of the basement's three rooms. There was a brilliant bluish flash and a sharp popping noise. I instinctively clenched my eyes shut and ducked my head, protecting it from what, I had no idea. Opening my eyes slowly, I saw that only half of the big empty room was lit. A bulb had blown.

"Gave up the fight, did ya?" I asked it. It didn't answer, thank goodness, but at that time of night, you never knew.

When I came back upstairs, I paused in the dining room. The sharp white moon was now centered in the piano window above the sideboard. I stood and looked at it for a long time with the laundry basket of clean, dry clothes propped on my right hip. What had that dream been about? It was more of a feeling, a memory, than a dream. With my free hand, I pressed my forehead between my eyebrows and gave myself a little head-clearing rub. I was getting tired of thinking about visions, dreams and sensations. I was tired. Period.

It was a little before four a.m., and I knew I couldn't go back to sleep even if I did head back up to bed. I had taken a long run the day before, and Asha was still asleep, so I turned to more mundane tasks to kill time. I could feel beady little eyes, tiny black letters and a mishmash of numbers boring into the back of my head. Putting down the laundry basket of clean running gear, mostly socks, I turned to face the source of the pressure.

The mail that Asha had set aside for me during the past busy weeks, some of it which was now almost a month old, was staring me down from the middle of the dining room table. I looked from the stack of envelopes to the basket of unpaired socks. Neither appealed to me, but the envelopes could at least be dealt with in an orderly fashion, top to bottom, whereas the socks were an unholy, random mess waiting to give me a backache as I bent over the basket peering for the other green-toed, yellow-striped mate. I left the laundry basket where it sat on the floor and pulled up a chair at the dining room table. The tabletop glowed silvery in the moonlight that shimmered through the leaded glass windows.

We so rarely used this dining room for its proper purpose anymore, not unless we were throwing a party or entertaining. Asha and I used to actually set the table, light candles and dine here, letting the dinner drag into the late evening as we talked and got to know one another better. But now it seemed we gravitated more toward the breakfast bar in the kitchen. It was closer to the action, and we had already successfully wooed each other with candlelit dinner conversation.

I turned on the dimmer switch so that a gentle light cascaded over the edges of the table. Later today, I promised myself, I would serve her dinner right here in the dining room like old times. Since her proposal, it was as if we were new again, in our younger relationship. Things hadn't ever really gotten old or stale between us, but this renewed energy I felt when I was around her lately brought into contrast the fact that we had gotten rather comfortable, maybe even complacent with each other.

I fanned through the stack of mail. I recognized almost all of the envelopes as statements telling me that I had automatically paid this bill or that bill. What a waste of paper. I shuffled through the rest of the envelopes. I should really consider going paperless on…a choked sob escaped my throat, which suddenly went dry.

The dining room chair tipped over behind me as I stood abruptly, holding one envelope and dropping all the rest. Guadalupe's steady, pretty handwriting grabbed my heart and twisted it until I thought it might break. I tried swallowing to bring an iota of moisture back to my throat, but it was useless. It seemed that all the moisture in my body had rushed to my head, there to press behind my eyes. Clutching the envelope to my chest, I began to walk through the house, moving through it without aim, almost without conscious thought.

Guadalupe. Guadalupe, you're here. I walked with her through the kitchen, back through the dining room, up the stairs through the bedrooms, down the stairs. Suddenly in need of fresh air, I slipped my bare feet into snow boots and walked with the envelope still pressed tight against my heart out the front door. The cold wind stung my face and hands. It howled between the houses and lifted my hair and hood from my shoulders, but the idea of her, of Guadalupe, being somehow contained within these papery confines warmed me. I cradled her as I walked around the side garden and into the back door. We came to rest on the kitchen floor, the cabinet that Asha had refinished when we bought the home pressing solidly at my back. I took a deep breath before looking at the envelope again. When I saw that it was really from her and not some wishful trick of my imagination, the corralled tears burst through their barbed-wire fences. It was a goddamn tear stampede.

When I recovered enough to control my shaking hands, I held the white envelope out before me and inspected it. One corner had a greasy black smear that ended in a tiny tear in the paper. I ran my fingertip along the tiny hole as I read the postmark. November 16, 2012. One week before Guadalupe died. What did she have to write to me one week before she died that she wasn't able to tell me in person? And what had prevented this letter from reaching me before now? I tore into the already ripped end of the envelope. I caught myself then, fearing I might damage the contents. I carefully finished freeing the folded paper within. A tiny scrap of red ribbon fell into my lap. I picked it up and brought it to my lips. Its satiny smoothness was comforting. I opened it and read Lupe's words.

Mi mitad de la Bodoquito, Cassie,
    I am in the hospital, and I doubt that I will be coming out. I write to you knowing that I will be departing soon,

but you should not ever feel that I have left you. I will never leave you. You are like my own child in my heart. Know that I love you like a mother loves her own.

I know that you love me as well, so please rest easy. I never wanted to seek a different path. You have brought so much light and warmth into my life that I never felt the need to wish for another. You brought me the ability to read English, when I can barely even read my own old language! You brought me your tears when you scraped your knee skin, you brought me treasures you found in the backyard, you brought me a passion for ball games, you brought me a deep understanding of human nature, and you brought me an expanded understanding of love. Thank you, Cassie, for these invaluable gifts.

I am about to change your past, and for this I feel content while having regrets. I feel these both at the same time, which is a little unsettling, but I do feel content because you will know that you truly are not alone in this world after I am gone. Yes, I know you have your mother and your father, and I hope that they will do right for you until the end, but you have even more than these two people who have been your parents. I feel regrets that I have not been brave enough to tell you this before now. I owe a great debt to your parents, so I have tried to be as respectful as I could be to them. At the same time, I have a great respect for you, so I am going to change your past, and maybe, even though I still do not believe that the future can be changed because it does not yet exist, I might change your future.

Now, if you are not sitting, please sit. If your dear Asha is nearby, please call her to you. If she is not nearby, you may read this anyway, as I know you will, but it might be easier with Asha at your side. Are you ready?

Was I ready? I could barely rip my eyes from Guadalupe's handwriting as it unraveled across this page, let alone go get Asha. Guadalupe knew me well, so it was against my better judgment to ignore her advice, but I was so hungry for her words that I started reading again, alone.

Mi Bodoquito, you have a sister. You were born a twin. You were born to a woman, not Margaret Windler, but to another woman who lived on the East Coast. I do not believe Lawrence Windler is your father, but I have never been certain of that. I do not know your mother's name, but I do know the address where she lived when I went with your parents to bring you into their family. The address I first met you at was 229 4th Avenue South, Myrtle Beach, South Carolina. You had just been born a few days before, and you had a tiny twin sister. Your sister's name is Polly. She cried like a storm when you were taken from her cradle, and you cried like a nestless bird when you heard her cry. Neither of you wanted to be without the other. It broke my heart, and I knew I'd never leave you because someday I would be the only one to tell you the truth.

I am so sorry that I waited so long to make that someday happen, but now you know. I know you will do what is right for you, *Bodoquito*. You always do what is right. You have been a wonderful child and now an incredible woman. To think that there is another half of you out there in the world comforts me and amazes me. This very small red ribbon was tied around your wrist to let your mother know which twin was which. You should keep it, as it is your very first belonging. Your sister wore a very small pink ribbon on her wrist. *Sana, sana, colita de rana, si no sanas hoy, sanarás mañana.*"

I will never leave you,
Your Lupe

CHAPTER TWENTY-FOUR

Run That by Me Again

I had not gone to get my dear Asha, as Guadalupe had often called her. Maybe I should have, but I didn't. Instead I had read the whole letter through alone, thinking that if seeing my parents arrested by the FBI a couple months ago didn't shock me into an early death, nothing else could, could it? Judging from my pulse and shortness of breath, I had my answer. Yes, this could be the final, ultimate shock.

I had a sister. A sister! And Margaret Windler was not my mother. I laughed and cried. I tipped my head up to try to force the tears back, but they streamed down from the corners of my eyes and ran into my hair at my temples. I laid down the letter and tiptoed up the stairs to see if Asha was awake, not really knowing what I would do or say if she had already woken up. I had a sister.

The thought sat in my head like a truth I always knew was there but couldn't completely formulate or admit to myself. I felt completely flabbergasted, yet I knew that deep down I was not surprised.

The feeling made me think of a story my colleague Andrea had told me. Andrea had been adopted from a Korean orphanage when she was seven years old. At the orphanage, she spoke and heard only Korean, but once her adoptive parents brought her to America, she spoke and heard only American English. But, on occasion, when she did happen to hear the Korean language being spoken, she *understood* it. She could never muster the language from the recesses of her childhood memories in order to speak it herself, but she understood it when she heard it. It was as if the language was there, waiting for her, in the deepest, most remote wrinkles of her gray matter.

I felt this new knowledge of my twin sister had been there, waiting for me in my brain—and my heart—all along. It only required Guadalupe's words to free it enough so that it could present itself clearly before me. I had *known* this truth.

Our bedroom was still darkened. Asha slept soundly; I could hear her purr-snoring from beneath the mountain of bedding. I wouldn't wake her yet. I had only half-processed Guadalupe's words. I needed more time on my own to think through this. I pressed my fingertips hard between my eyebrows and tried to take a deep breath. My lungs were constricted, though, and I felt that a deep breath might only unleash a howling sob.

I held the stairway railing tightly as I made my way back down the stairs. I could run. That would sort everything out. From the clean clothesbasket, I put together a running outfit, grabbed my shoes and a Windbreaker from beside the front door and hit the winter streets.

Despite the icy frost, my shoes made no noise on the pavement and my breathing was so silent that it was as if I wasn't even there. Creating a slight breeze in my wake, thinking loud, crashing thoughts, I dashed invisible through Minneapolis.

I had a sister. *Have* a sister. My other half. Where is she? Why did Guadalupe wait to tell me now? Why not years ago? Did she think I wouldn't handle it well if she had told me earlier? No, she knows me. Knew me. Did she have such a heavy sense of commitment to my parents that she thought it was important to keep their secret? And how was it that her letter hadn't arrived earlier? What the hell? Who were my parents anyway? Not this doctor and his appearances-only wife. And who did this all make *me*?

A loud honking penetrated my personal bubble. I veered to the right and my eyes came out of their hundred-mile stare and into focus on an MTC bus that was empty save for the driver. What a waste, empty buses. What a waste, not knowing I had a sister.

Was that true, though? Hadn't I felt it all along? That I was missing a part of myself? Yes. I had. But I had never let myself think it was a sister, a twin that I was missing. I had chalked it up to the cold, sterile world that my parents inhabited.

I allowed myself to examine that idea more closely—and discovered that conclusion wasn't as accurate as I had thought it to be, either. My father had been warm, he'd been kind and he'd paid some attention to me. My mother, she was the cold, scientific one. My father was just a slave to her whims. No, not whims. Normal people had whims. My mother had calculations, not whims. *I* was a calculation for her.

I pounded around another corner. I had a twin. And I had another mother and father. Had had? What had happened that we were not all together? Was my twin still alive? Did she look like me? Was she a runner too? Did her mother, *our* mother love her? Had she had a proper childhood with smiles that reached her parents' eyes and hugs that happily whooshed the air from her laughing lungs? Would she want to know me? Tears, stinging in the cold, streamed into my hair as I ran quietly, intensely, not knowing where I was going except forward...

I ran until I knew. Until Linda Crespo's stories about the twins in her research came flooding back over me, threatening to drown me. Then I stopped.

She did look like me, only she looked older.

She wanted to know me.

She needed to know me. She needed to know me *now*.

I looked to the nearest street sign. I was at Nicollet and 2nd. My sister. How was it that she needed me? What was wrong? The man in her kitchen, Axel. That was what was wrong. His face, glowering and bitter, filled my mind. I tried to push him out, but he was lodged in there. I was already almost out of breath, but what little air I had left my lungs, as if the image of Axel left no room for anything else. I bent over and rested my hands on my knees. Stars dotted the backs of my closed eyelids as I inhaled as deeply as I could. I exhaled slowly. I could fix this. I could. I inhaled one more big breath, stood up, and opened my eyes. I let my feet find their way home as I mentally wrote the checklist that would have me on a plane to Myrtle Beach by tomorrow evening, fully packed and prepared to face this fear that something horrible was about to happen to my sister. To Polly.

CHAPTER TWENTY-FIVE

Leaving Asha

"What do you mean you have a sister?" Asha asked as I blurted out bits of the story on my way upstairs. She followed me to our bedroom, where I heaved our suitcase onto the bed and started throwing clothes into it. I had already booked a flight for 6:15 p.m. that same night, much sooner than I had expected to be able to get one. I hoped, as I pulled random scraps of outfits off hangers and tossed them toward the gaping suitcase, that Asha would understand. I hoped she wouldn't think I had lost my mind, even though I considered the possibility myself.

"I have a twin sister," I repeated. I stopped, took a deep breath, looked at the contents of the suitcase and decided against bringing a suitcase at all because I didn't want to waste time fetching it at baggage claim once I landed. Time was important now. I would take a backpack instead. If I had to be there for more than a day or two, I'd buy whatever I might need.

"Right, you told me," Asha said. "But *how*? What happened?"

"I don't know...!" I wailed.

I sat down hard on the bed. I cradled my temples in my hands, my hair falling between my fingers to my knees under my elbows. I cried. My tears joined the pooling hair on my knees. There was so much time before the flight, so much time to just wait and *wait*. I couldn't do anything until I got there, and the sooner I got there, the safer my twin, my other half would be. I knew now why I was having these visions. They weren't of my life; they were of *hers*.

The bed dipped next to me under Asha's weight. I felt her hand on my back and her hip next to mine.

"Cass, what happened?"

"I have a sister. My mother and father bought me from some woman, from my real mother, out on the East Coast," I said between tears and hiccups. I took a gaspy, deep breath and continued. "I've been having these visions…thought it was me, but it was her. Guadalupe sent a letter."

"Guadalupe?" Asha's voice rose an octave. I felt her leg tense up next to mine.

"Guadalupe." I hiccupped.

"Now?"

"I don't know," I said.

"When did you get the letter?" Asha's voice was patient.

"It was on the table in the pile, but I only saw it now, this morning. And then I ran to make sense of it, came home, booked a flight and by then you were awake," I said. I hoped she wasn't upset with me for not waking her as soon as I read it.

"Oh," she said, "that explains the lack of a runner's buffet breakfast." She didn't take her hand from my back and she'd made an attempt at a joke, so I assumed she wasn't too upset, if at all.

"She must have had a friend send it after she was gone or something," I said. I felt Asha relax a bit.

"And?" she pushed.

"You can read it. It's downstairs, dining room, no, kitchen, on the floor, I think, " I told her. I sniffled hard.

She kissed the back of my head and said she'd be right back. The bed sprang up with her exit. I rubbed my forehead, trying to collect myself enough to keep it together until I could get on the plane and get to…Polly. Guadalupe's letter said her name was Polly. Such a funny, old-fashioned name, Polly. Polly

Windler. No, that wouldn't be it, would it? She'd have a different last name. She'd have...she'd have my real last name. What was my last name? Unless she was married, then she'd have a different name. That fucking ogre better not be her husband. He couldn't be her husband; she'd be smarter than to marry him, wouldn't she? Well? She was a carnival ride operator. That didn't mean she wasn't smart, though. Did it? She always had a classic literature paperback stuck in a pocket. My heart ached for her.

I sat up, and the dull, achy tear hangover clung to the back of my skull. The bedside clock read 10:03. I had too much time to kill. Asha's head appeared above the hallway floor, then her shoulders, and finally her hips, knees and feet as she climbed the stairs.

"Oh my god, Cass," she breathed. She was still finishing the letter, or perhaps rereading it, when she sat down next to me on the bed again. "Oh my god."

"I know," was all I could say.

She held the letter in her lap and looked at me. "What are you going to do?" she asked.

"I'm going out there," I said. Asha's face held concern for me. What did she think I was going to do? Why else would I have been packing? Even though I wasn't going to take the suitcase after reconsidering baggage claim time, why else would I have packed?

"I understand," Asha said, "that this is a sudden...discovery for you, but why the rush?"

"Why the rush?" My voice sounded shrill. I lowered it to a modicum of normalcy, and I said, "I have to help her," failing to consider the fact that I'd never told Asha about the visions I was having. This was all new to her.

Asha's response was to raise an eyebrow at me.

"I've been seeing her, my twin," I began. How would I not sound crazy in all this? Should I even be telling Asha about the visions? But I had already started, so I should finish. "I've been having these...visions of her...and she needs help. There's some asinine guy who's pushing her around, and there's a gun. I have to...need to help, I think. No, I know."

"You've been having visions?"

"Yeah."

"Why didn't you tell me?" Asha's eyes were sharp.

"Ash, I didn't want you to think I was crazy…" I attempted to explain.

She cut me off. "What? Like you are having dreams of somebody pushing around a woman you don't know?" I couldn't blame her for not getting it; I barely got it, but she didn't have to get angry about it, did she?

"Yeah, no. I'm seeing it, only I thought it was me. She looks like me. I thought it was my future."

"You're seeing it? Not dreaming it?"

"Right. No. Well, usually I see it, I envision it, but I guess there have been some dreams as well." I sounded crazy even to myself.

"And now you're going to go find her and…do what? Get the guy?"

It sounded stupid when she said it, but yes, that was what I was planning on doing. "Yes," I answered.

"How long have you…been seeing her?"

"Since fall," I said and hung my head. "I should have told you."

Asha bit her lower lip and nodded once. She took a deep, audible breath.

"Did I ever tell you that my *last* girlfriend *never* missed my award ceremony?" she asked without mirth in her eyes.

"Oh, Asha, I am so sorry," I said. I had forgotten that tomorrow night was the night she was being presented with the Twin Cities Community Builder Award.

I knew she didn't know what to make of all this. I was sorry that I hadn't told her when I started having the visions; that might have made it easier for her now. But I only was able to put it all together with the help of Lupe's letter. I only finally understood it just now myself. And I hoped she'd understand and forgive me for not being there tomorrow night.

CHAPTER TWENTY-SIX

Second Attempt

The girl behind the counter snapped her gum at me.

"That'll be eleven and a quarter," she said with a bright British clip to her words. I wondered if it was a real accent or if it was an assumed one. What would draw a kid from England to the Midwest? Certainly not her job as a cashier at the airport newsstand. I handed her a twenty. She counted my change and handed it over to me.

I scooped up my magazine, bottled water and pack of gum. Eleven and a quarter did not go very far these days. I felt old as soon as the phrase "these days" went through my mind. I felt old from hearing that my father, who probably wasn't even really my father, had falsified data for some corporate bribe. From discovering that the woman who claimed to be my mother had really just used me as a merit badge on her doctor's do-gooder wife sash and as a mascot for a bogus charity. As well as from learning that I had half of me missing since a few days after our birth. I was tired. I knew I wasn't thinking straight, and I knew things were going to explode soon. I just hoped I made it to her, to Polly, in time.

The wait for boarding seemed to last forever. I pulled Lupe's letter from the interior breast pocket of my jacket. I inspected the November sixteenth postmark on its envelope. Why had it taken so long to get to me? Had it been stuck at the bottom of the letter carrier's bag? Wedged in the mailbox, out of sight and out of reach? I pressed the envelope to my lips and then tucked it back into my jacket, against my heart. There'd been no date on the letter itself and she'd written that she was already in the hospital. Had Guadalupe written it on the same date it was posted? Or had she written it before that—just to have it ready and waiting to be mailed?

My mind was caught up in eddies of disbelief and relief and recognition. And fear. If I were honest, fear was the biggest eddy I was swirling around in at the moment. Feeling as if I might drown, as soon as I got into my seat on the plane I dug into my bag for the magazine I had bought. Perhaps I could pull my mind out of its whirlpool and into…what magazine had I picked up? *Pet Fancy*? Seriously? I hadn't even looked at the title at the newsstand. I'd only known that I'd need some sort of print medicine to ease my misery over having to endure the real, clock time interlude on the plane when all I wanted to do was get to the coast and make sure my sister was safe.

A cockatoo with bulging black eyes raised his lemon yellow crest at me from the cover of the magazine. It could have been worse; I could have blindly chosen a…yeah, it couldn't really have been worse. Just about any other magazine would have been more appealing. I had no interest in reading about how intelligent cockatoos were, how unhealthy a raw diet can be for domestic dogs or how to toilet train my cat. I tried to picture Wasabi perched on the edge of the toilet seat. No, I still had no desire to read anything in this magazine.

I stared into the trusting, intelligent eyes of a big golden retriever in an ad for an organic dog food and wondered if Asha would forgive me my humongous transgression. I should have told her about the visions so much earlier. The problem was I had just kept thinking they'd go away—that the last one I'd had would be the last one ever. And I should have told her right away what Art had shared with me about my parents so that she wasn't blindsided when they were taken into custody. Then again, on that one I might cut myself some slack. I had known what Art said, and I was still caught off guard by the FBI taking them that night.

Asha was probably out shopping for a normal girlfriend as I sat waiting for the plane to take off. Or maybe she was thinking that Beth, Esme's Elizabeth, despite all her flirty faults, would make a better partner than some delusional woman who'd been raised by white-collar criminals. I pushed the thought from my head and broke eye contact with the paper dog staring up at me from the glossy magazine.

I closed the pages and turned to look outside. I was sandwiched between a man and a woman, but we were in front of the wing, so I had a decent view out the window. We were still on the ground. I watched the crew loading suitcases into the plane parked next to ours. They worked like a well-oiled machine, throwing luggage into the gaping maw at the side of the plane, tooling around in little train-like vehicles and motioning to one another in a cryptic sign language. The workers reminded me of ants. They all knew their job, they were all good at it and they probably had had no life-changing surprises sprung on them in the last week.

Wait. That wasn't fair. Ants always had surprises. They had to deal with the random destruction of their dwellings by big feet and curious snouts and sudden downpours or freezes—although they probably sensed the weather things coming. Okay, so maybe the workers encountered some surprises now and again as well—though not surprises like dealing with luggage that was too big to fit or suddenly having to load a school bus instead of a plane. The airlines saw to it that things ran pretty smoothly, I guessed. I would bet that not one ant and likely none of the workers either had discovered recently that they didn't belong to the family they thought they belonged to.

Had *she* known about *me* her whole life? Had her mother, our mother, told her I existed? I remembered then—the vision I'd had before Guadalupe's funeral and the conversation that had taken place between them. Our mother had told Polly she wasn't alone. That was me they'd been speaking of. My sister knew of me, but she'd only been told recently. Still, why hadn't she tried to find me? For that matter, why had my mother never found me? And what was happening to my sister right now? I knew she needed me, and not just because of the visions that were scary as hell when that Axel guy was around. I could feel it. I could feel the pull from her.

The flight to Charlotte got in later than expected, turning the short layover there into a blur. I had to sprint to my connecting flight, my backpack whapping me in the kidneys with every step of my run. It was good, actually, to have something concrete to worry about.

I got settled in my seat for the second leg of my journey, again smack-dab between another man and a woman. That was fine with me; maybe they would be chatty and help take my mind off this new reality. No luck. As we began the ascent, they both pulled out reading material. I was left alone with my questions again.

"Would you like anything to drink?" The flight attendant's voice swirled around in my whirlpool of thoughts for a moment before it separated itself and rose to the top.

"What? Uhm, no, thank you," I said, and then I had to change my answer. "Wait, yes, I'm sorry, I would like a vodka tonic, please."

The flight attendant nodded. I handed her my cash and she handed me a plastic glass of clear liquid and transparent cubes and a miniature blue bottle of Skyy vodka.

It was funny how suddenly I was desperate for a drink. Even after I added the liquor, the beverage remained translucent—like a glass of nothing. Right now, though, I was depending on it to still the incessant questions milling about in my mind. I took a long drink and drained half the plastic cup, the ice cubes sloshing dangerously close to the edge. I would have slammed the entire beverage down, I think, if I had not been concerned about what the other passengers might think. I looked at the man on my left. He was reading a paperback. The woman on my right was reading an electronic book. Seeing that neither seemed aware of me, I did chug the remainder of my drink, careful this time to keep the ice in the cup. Calm flowed over me for a moment, so I leaned against the seatback and closed my eyes.

With a dull, painful thud, my ears reacted to the pressure change. I reopened my eyes and swallowed hard to clear my ears. I thought of Polly crying out when Axel kicked her ribs. What was she doing right now? Was she in trouble as I tried to get to her? Would I make it in time?

I needed to have another vision of her, I thought—then I would stop worrying. I would know that she was safe, maybe joking around with her carnival friends with a copy of *The Odyssey* peeking out of her back pocket. Or maybe at home alone, getting ready for bed, looking skinny in her faded pajamas.

I should have ordered two vodka tonics. How had the other visions started? What had triggered them? They had come at random times, I thought, and in random places. I closed my eyes again and thought very hard about Polly. I tried to picture her, called to her in my mind. But nothing happened. There was no vision of her whatsoever.

I sighed and gave up. Reaching for my backpack, which was stowed under the seat in front of me, I rummaged around until I found my magazine. Okay, *Pet Fancy*, let's see what you can do for me.

For thirteen full minutes, I was able to educate myself about the intelligence of cockatoos and the dangers of raw dog food. I avoided the "toilet train your cat" article because, frankly, I liked being fifty percent of the toilet traffic in my house. I didn't want to think about sharing with Wasabi.

To make up for that selfishness, I paged through the back of the magazine to see if there were any products being advertised that Wasabi might appreciate. There was an interactive, multi-level cat perch that looked entertaining, but Wasabi was getting old and probably wouldn't use the upper levels much at all, and that's where all the interactive action was according to the ad's picture. The little pearls that could be glued on to cats' toenails were cute, but, reading on, I discovered that they were intended to prevent kitty from shredding the couch and curtains. Wasabi had her nails, but had never dug into anything other than her scratching post. No pearls then.

Aha! There it was. A heated fleece cat cave beckoned to me from the glossy page. This would make up for not toilet training Wasabi. She could have her own cat cave for a mere $229 plus tax and shipping. Not bad, really.

I tried to stretch my legs and promptly rammed my shin into the seat in front of me. Damn it. I should have gone first class, but I never even thought of it. The price I'd pay for my own comfort was much higher than that $229. I closed my eyes and let my head rest against the seat. I took off my glasses and rubbed my forehead, keeping my eyes closed...

"Polly, call me as soon as you get this," pleaded a woman who looked like a much older version of me. I knew this was my mother, my real mother. She held a cell phone to her ear.

"I just have a real bad feeling, sweetheart, and I'm worried for you," she said into the phone. I could hear the love and concern in her voice, and I ached for her. She opened her mouth to say more, but at that point there was an almighty banging and she dropped the phone. She turned around, looking beyond the vantage point from which I could see her, her light green eyes huge with panic. The cell phone spun on its back on the counter behind her. The banging started again.

"I know the money's here, bitch!" a man's voice bellowed. I tried to lift my eyelids, but couldn't. There was a deafening crash like a door being forced open and slammed into a wall.

"Axel! It's not here, there's no money!" the woman—my mother—pleaded. I felt a horrible chill rush through me, and then Axel was there, grabbing my mother and throwing her aside against the countertop. She cried out as her hip struck the cabinet.

"Shut up, Annie," Axel growled. "I know it's here. I'm going to find it."

"There's no money. She's telling you the truth—there's nothing she's hiding from you!"

"You don't know anything, do you," Axel sneered, his face contorted with rage. He lunged toward her. His blue work shirt, open to reveal a gray T-shirt beneath, flared out on the sides with the burst of his speed. My mother backed against the counter, but her face showed strength. Courage.

"I know that if you don't—oh!" She cried out as he grabbed her by the shoulders and smashed her backward, her head hitting the upper cabinets, once, twice before she fell to the ground. I heard her cry and then moan, but I couldn't see her any longer because the table, covered with a cheery yellow floral-patterned fabric, was in the way.

Noooooooo! I cried out in my head. I screamed silently for my mother. My mother, Annie, my real mother. No!

"You," Axel snarled. He pulled a small, metallic gun from the back of his pants. It was the gun from the drawer in the nightstand. He pointed it at her, at my real mother. "You don't know anything now!" He fired the gun, and I felt it in the base of my throat; I *felt* it.

"And pretty soon neither will your daughter."

I heard yelling and watched Axel as he rammed the gun down the back of his pants again and left. I knew my mother, whom I'd never even properly met, was dead. A part of my heart was cold. The yelling got nearer, and less than a minute after Axel left the room, two strangers entered.

"Annie!" the woman called. The man looked left and then right, not seeing what he needed to see.

"Annie, are you here?" the woman called as she walked to the other side of the table. She looked down, dropped out of sight and began the wailing for which I felt the need so desperately in my soul. I still couldn't open my eyes, and I could not cry out. I tried to force myself to move, to call out, to get help for Polly because Axel was on his way to her, but I could do nothing…

CHAPTER TWENTY-SEVEN

Polly

All at once, the entire room bounced and bounced again. My eyes flew open and I saw passengers preparing to leave the plane. As soon as I could, I grabbed my backpack, started fumbling in the side pocket for my phone, and rammed my way through the plane to the exit.

My phone took forever to turn on. I decided to call the police en route. Outside the airport, I grabbed a taxi, told the driver to take me to Sandy's Sand Bar and Café and told him it was a matter of life and death.

"Of course it is," he said, but he sped out to the highway a few miles over the speed limit.

I dialed nine-one-one.

"This is the nine-one-one operator. Is this an emergency?" a woman's voice, surprisingly calm, said into my ear.

"Yes, this is an emergency!" I cried. "I need help at Sandy's Sand Bar and Café. There's going to be trouble for my sister. Axel has a gun, and he's going there now—he might already be there!" I took a quick breath, expecting to have to keep urging her on, but she cut me off.

"And what is your name?" she asked.

"My name? My name is Cassie Windler, well, yes, Cassie Windler, and my sister is Polly, and she's in trouble!"

"Okay, try to remain calm," she urged. Remain calm? That was giving me more credit than I deserved. The taxi cab driver's eyes met mine in his rearview mirror. I saw he was concerned. Whether it was concern for me or for my sister or for himself, I didn't know or care.

"Right. A guy named Axel just killed our mother, Annie… and now he's going to shoot Polly, my sister."

"Cassie, we have two squad cars on their way to Sandy's Sand Bar. What is your location?"

"I don't know. I'm in a cab on the way—"

"Highway Fifteen and Third Avenue South, we're two blocks away now," the cab driver said to me. I repeated the location to the 911 operator. I started crying. I was so scared for my sister that I couldn't do anything else.

"Ssshhh…the police are on their way, Cassie," the operator said.

I could see the squad cars one block away. Two cops were standing outside the weather-beaten blue building of my visions.

"Thank you, I see them," I said to the operator. I ended the call and launched myself out of the cab almost before it stopped.

The younger cop sensed my panic. "Peej? What's wrong? What's going on?" he asked.

"No, I'm not Peej. But she needs you to get up there! She needs help!"

Both cops eyed me, but the younger of the two believed me when I said we needed to rush. He brushed past the older cop who had started sauntering toward the corner and managed to double-time it down the other side of the block, halfway down the street to a rickety door with a gouge in the screen. I barely had time to realize that I had seen the door in the peeling, faded blue building before. I recognized it from an early vision I'd had. The younger cop blasted into the bar with me close on his heels.

"Sandy, P.J. here?" the cop called over his shoulder to the blond bartender without waiting for her response.

He slowed to a trot and shoved chairs aside as he made his way to the back of the bar. I followed, only to have the older cop rush past me. He was in better shape than I'd thought to be able to catch up to us that quickly. The two of them turned a corner, and I heard the ricochet of their shoes' soles smacking the unseen stairs before I rounded the same corner and pounded up the same stairs. My eyes were so full of scared tears that I had to hold the banister the entire way up. I was surprised to hear breathing behind me. I turned just enough to see the big blond woman from behind the bar clambering up the steps behind me.

"They're both up there, Jason," she called past me. "They're fighting already although Axel just got here. He's in a piss-poor mood tonight."

The bashing open of the wooden door at the top of the small landing made me cry out. The silent hustling and then the hollering that followed made me fear the worst.

"Back away from her, Axel!" a voice bellowed. "Back away from her!"

"She had it coming to her—bitch stole all my money, she stole my life! She had it comin'!" The rage in Axel's voice was palpable.

"It's all over, Axel," said a different, younger-sounding voice, trying another tactic. "It's all over, drop the gun, put your hands in the air where I can see 'em both and back into the other room."

"You don't get it do you?" Axel snarled. "You don't get it! She had you all fooled!" His voice reverberated through the staircase where we waited. My heart pounded and pulsed in my ears, threatening to become loud enough to drown out the yelling.

"Is P.J. okay?" Sandy called.

"Stay back, Sandy, keep 'er back on the stairs. Or better, go downstairs," the older cop yelled to us.

"That's good, Axel, keep backing up, but you gotta drop your gun," the younger cop's voice suggested that his bravado was wavering. "Keep going, Axel, everything's gonna be okay." He didn't sound very sure about this. "Yeah, this is Unit One, we need an ambulance upstairs at the Sand Bar." There were scuffling footsteps on the floor.

"Good job, Ax, good job, now drop your gun," the older cop said. I could tell they'd entered another room from how their voices sounded. "It's all over," the older cop continued in a soothing monotone, "you did what you came here to do, it's all over—"

As he said this, I gasped. I grasped the railing as my knees began to buckle. A sob escaped me. I felt the bartender's arm encircle my ribcage from behind me, heard her tell me she had me and then I knew my fears were founded. With my body held firmly to hers, she pushed into the apartment and into the kitchen I knew from my visions.

"This doesn't even involve you!" Axel was still raging.

"Put it down, Axel. Drop it. Drop it now!" From the other room, the young cop suddenly sounded older than he had seconds ago.

I felt the bartender soften behind me, and she let go of my ribcage. I looked down in front of us, and my heart shattered. Beside the kitchen counter, lying on the floor was my twin. I felt my entire body go cold. I dropped to my knees beside my sister's body. I saw my hands, as if in a dream, go to the sides of her face, my face. The left side was sticky and her hair was matted with blood, which I saw was pooling under her neck when I picked her up by the shoulders and held her to me. I sobbed and rocked her, holding her head to the side of mine.

"No, no, no," Sandy crooned, still behind me.

I tuned out the voices and pounding footsteps that were thundering up the staircase. I tuned out the violent shouting in the other room. I even managed to tune out most of the noise of the two gunshots that blasted, one after the other, seemingly all around us, all around my sister and me. She was still warm.

CHAPTER TWENTY-EIGHT

Happy Birthday to Us

Polly—P.J.—awoke on our birthday. Well, almost. She came out of her coma on February twenty-eighth. We were Leaplings, so we didn't actually *have* a birthday this year. Babies born on February twenty-ninth are so unlucky. Then again, on second thought, perhaps we are luckier than others. Every four years, I'd have a very special birthday, on the correct date, and then, for three years in a row, I'd have two days of celebration that bookended that ephemeral day, my birthday. *Our* birthday. I wondered how Polly had celebrated all those days.

When she awoke, I was perched on a chair next to her hospital bed. My arms were wrapped around my legs and my knees were drawn up under my chin. I had been by her side almost nonstop for five days as she lingered on the edge of her coma. I had only left three times to shower quickly and change clothes at the hotel room Asha had gotten for us less than a mile from the hospital. Asha had flown out the day after I had—right after her award ceremony. Each time I'd left, either Sandy, the blond bartender, or Kris, Polly's best friend, had sat vigil with

Polly. But now it was just Asha and I who watched Polly's face for any sign of change.

"Oh!" I exclaimed when I saw that Polly's eyes, so much like my own eyes, were opening. I smiled hard through the tears that began streaming down my face. I unfolded my body and stood up a little. I grabbed her hand and arm, watching out for the IV tubes and needles in the back of her hand and inside her elbow. Asha stood up on the other side of the bed.

"You're back. You're here," I told her. "You're here, P.J." I gripped her arm so tightly that I feared I might injure her further, but I couldn't stop myself. "You're okay. I'm Cassie, your twin. We're here."

She stared at me and nodded. She tried to smile, I think, or to say something, but her lips were dry despite the lip balm and ice chips that Asha, P.J.'s nurses and I had been religiously administering for days. Her eyes were so bright. I didn't expect that. I couldn't look away. It was as if some heavy invisible chain was connecting us as we looked at each other.

"Here, drink, it's water," Asha said quietly. She sounded as if she were sort of strangling on held-back tears. This made me cry even harder. I was so relieved. I don't think I had had any idea how scared and stressed I was while waiting for P.J. to come to until she actually woke up. Then it all hit me at once. I cried over her as Asha helped her to take several small sips of water. P.J. cleared her throat. Asha held the water to her lips for one last sip, and for this sip, P.J. raised the hand that I wasn't clutching for dear life to hold the cup for herself. Now she could properly smile at me.

"It's been a very long time. It's nice to see you again, Cassie," she whispered through her huge grin.

Asha laughed, but her laughter turned to hiccupping, teary sobs like mine. I managed to get my arms around P.J. without upsetting any tubes or machines for our first real hug in ages. I held her so hard to me. I didn't want to ever let her go. There was a bustling behind me, and I knew that others had come into the room. I heard Asha telling someone that P.J. had just woken up and that she had spoken and that P.J.'s sense of humor was intact. I knew the nurses or doctor or whoever had come in would want to check up on P.J., so I eased her back onto her bed.

Her eyes were so, so bright, as if this five-day coma had been a refreshing little nap. She actually looked healthier here than she had looked in many of my visions. Her hair had been shampooed the first day she arrived so that the doctors could examine the head wound where Axel had bashed her with the butt of his gun. She had several stitches above her left ear, and even though they had had to shave her hair away from the wound, it wasn't as pronounced as I thought it would be. Hair was nothing; it would grow back.

And she looked a bit more filled out, not so scrawny and underfed. Her color was higher than it had been in my visions. Maybe there was something magical about being in a coma. Or perhaps it was the IV fluids. More likely it was being away from an abusive asshole, which gave her the peace she needed in order to mend. Funny that getting bashed upside the head with the butt of a gun would allow her to become a healthier being.

The doctor asked P.J. questions to ensure that she was processing well, and then she told P.J. that she'd undergo a neurological test later to make sure everything was perfect, but that she was checking out quite well from what the doctor could determine. P.J. had already had an EEG to determine what had caused the coma, and nothing had turned up in the test. She had been on a ventilator for the first three days but then was breathing well enough on her own to do without. The doctor had said it was likely just swelling in the brain that caused the coma.

Neither Asha nor I could stop staring at P.J. as the doctor and nurse tended to her. I wondered what Asha was thinking. I tore my eyes away from P.J. for a moment to raise an eyebrow at Asha and smile at her.

"She just looks so much like you," Asha said. She came to my side, walking around behind the doctor, who was flashing a thin light into P.J.'s eyes, and the nurse, who was taking notes.

"I know," I said as Asha wrapped her arm around my lower back.

"What's it like," she asked, "to meet her finally?" I didn't get to answer because the doctor looked up at me just then.

"Your sister is out of the woods," the doctor said. "I let her know how she came to be here—that she had been attacked and hit on the side of the head with a gun." The doctor looked hard at me. She hadn't told P.J. anything else, I gathered, from her look. "She's doing well, it seems. We're going to keep her here for at least another twenty-four hours for a couple more tests and for observation, and then we can evaluate her leaving." The doctor tipped her head to P.J. and said, "You take it easy on the soup the nurses are going to bring for you in a few minutes. Stop eating before you feel full, okay."

"I can't make any promises," my sister said. Her throat still sounded raw. She smiled.

"Funny now," the doctor responded, "but it won't feel funny later." She winked at P.J. and left.

The silence after the doctor left only lasted a second.

"So what did I miss?" P.J. asked, still smiling. My heart crashed from the top of the world to just about the bottom. I was going to have to tell P.J. that her mother, our mother, was dead. I didn't even think to ask the doctor about how to or when to do this. How could I not let her know immediately?

"Well," I pulled a chair back to her bedside. Asha pulled a chair over to her other side. I sat down. Asha didn't. "I'm your sister, your twin, Cassie." P.J. held out her hand in order to shake mine.

"I'm P.J. A few months ago Mom told me you existed… somewhere. Nice to meet you again, finally," she laughed and weakly pumped my hand up and down.

"And this is my partner, my fiancée, Asha," I said. I didn't even worry about coming out as a lesbian to my twin because I was so dreading telling her about her mother.

She held out her hand for Asha to shake. "I'm pleased as punch to meet you," she said. Her East Coast accent was endearing.

"And I couldn't be happier to meet you, P.J. I am so glad you are awake," Asha said. "Excuse me, I have to go check on a timing issue. I'll be right back." Asha looked at me to see if I understood what she meant by "timing issue." God, I thought. Asha is the perfect woman. She was going to go check to see if the shock of hearing of her mother's death would be too much for P.J. at this point. I nodded, and Asha zipped out of the room.

"How are you feeling?" I asked P.J.

"I don't know," she responded. "I feel comfortable in my body, my head feels okay and I'm very surprised that you are here. What happened?"

"I...uh..." I tried to think of something to stall, but I couldn't. Where was Asha? I looked into P.J.'s eyes and thought hard about how to tell her. I didn't have any idea how to do this. At all. I took a deep breath and was about to say something, anything, when she spoke.

"Cassie, I know Mom's gone," she said very quietly. Her raspy drawling accent made me love her even more. I began crying again.

"I am sorry, P.J.," I sniffed. "I am so sorry."

"It's okay," she said, and she squeezed my hand. "It's okay." Why was she consoling me? And how did she know? I looked at her through my tears.

"I think she told me goodbye while I was out," she began, "and I know that sounds crazy, but I kind of remember her visiting me and telling me that she loved us both, and that everything will be okay." P.J. was now crying with me. "That does sound crazy, doesn't it?" She laughed through her tears and brought the hand that wasn't squeezing mine up to her throat. I poured her another little cup of water, and she gratefully swallowed some of it down.

"Do you know I could see you?" I asked before I even thought about the words coming out of my mouth. "I saw you at work, I saw you in your kitchen, and I saw you with that... with..." I couldn't even bring myself to say Axel's name.

"With that asshole," she supplied. It sounded nicer than I felt it to be when she said it with her soft drawl. "I wish he were dead!" she spat out. "I know he's to blame, for Mom being gone, and I know...I know it's wrong to wish ill on anyone...but he's so mean." She looked at me to see my response, so I shook my head, and then I nodded. She knew what I meant. "He told me he killed her before he hit me with his gun," she said and then cleared her throat. She took another sip of water. "I thought he was messing with me...until she visited to say goodbye." She pressed her lips together as tears coursed down her cheeks. "I hate him!" she wailed.

Asha came back in the room at that point. She stood behind me, placed both hands firmly on my shoulders and leaned over me.

"We're not supposed to upset her," Asha whispered in my ear. She stood back up and squeezed my shoulders a little.

"P.J.? He's gone," I said. "It's all over; he's dead."

"What happened?"

"He wouldn't drop the gun. The one he hit you in the head with. He wouldn't drop it when the cops told him to," I began. "Then he shot one of the cops in the shoulder—he's okay—a cop named Brandt?" She nodded. Axel had shot the young cop. "Then the other cop, Officer Dearing, shot Axel. In the chest."

"Ooohhhh..." she exhaled.

"He died in your apartment. The paramedics took you downstairs and brought you here, and then they went back for him. But I think he was...I think he died before the paramedics even left with you...I was so worried for you that I didn't pay much..."

My voice trailed off. She let go of my hand to cover her face with both hands as she sobbed. Through the thin hospital bed linen, I patted her thigh as she cried. A nurse came in and stood at the foot of the bed. I didn't make eye contact with the nurse; I was certain I was in trouble. I just waited for P.J. to stop crying. I patted her thigh and made shushing sounds to her.

"I'm okay," P.J.'s voice was muffled in her hands. She sniffled loudly, pulled up the bedsheet to wipe her eyes and then reached for tissues to blow her nose. The loud honking made her laugh at herself. She said, "Oh my God, what else could happen now?" I wondered if she were on the verge of hysteria. The nurse, Asha and I all watched her carefully.

"I really am okay," she reassured us. "I've had a few days to come to terms with Mom," she said, not bothering to explain to Asha or the nurse. "And fifty percent of those tears just now were tears of relief; the other fifty percent were pure sadness over the time I spent with that hateful man." Her voice quivered. "He's gone." She looked thoughtful for a moment. "I feel like I can finally breathe," she said to me.

"Me too."

CHAPTER TWENTY-NINE

Leapfrogs

During the following day, a few major decisions were made. The first one touched my heart so profoundly that I can't even begin to describe how it made me feel. To begin with, I had a sister. I finally had real family, and a twin, no less. The day before she was discharged from the Intensive Care Unit, my sister asked me to call her Polly.

"It's my real name," she said, "and Mom used to call me Polly. If she can't and you call me P.J., then there is no one who will ever call me by my real name."

I wondered if she was the second born as I saw how guileless she was in this request. She looked so young and innocent sitting cross-legged on her hospital bed in the green-and-orange-striped pajamas Asha had bought for her at a nearby shopping mall. I was saddened for a few moments by the fact that we should have spent countless hours in our pajamas on our beds sharing secrets and laughter as we grew up together. We had missed out on so much. I had, of course, happily agreed to calling P.J. Polly.

The second big decision was that Polly would come live with us, at least for the time being. It was an oddly made decision. I had never thought anything else, but I had not yet mentioned it to Asha or to Polly.

Asha had said, "You'll be coming to live with us, in our house," to Polly and her doctor after her doctor had asked if there was someone who could look in on her every now and then.

And Polly simply said, "Thank you. I'd be thrilled to." And that was that. We had the empty third floor of the big Victorian, so room would be no problem.

The third decision was harder. It was Polly's decision more so than mine. Officer Daniel Brandt, with his wounded shoulder immobilized in a sling, came to talk to both Polly and me right before Polly was discharged.

"Peej," he said from the hallway just beyond the doorway to Polly's room. "Peej, how are you?"

"Come in, Daniel, hi, I'm good," Polly said. "How are you?" Polly attempted to get up off the bed to embrace Daniel, but he rushed into the room holding out his good arm to dissuade her from rising. He grabbed her in a one-armed hug and held her.

"Thank you, Daniel, thank you," Polly said into Daniel's uniformed, shot shoulder. "Thank you so much!"

"Peej," Daniel said, his voice constricted, "I'm so sorry we didn't do anything earlier, before...we had no idea...I had no idea it was so bad, that he was so bad."

I had to look away from them. I rolled my eyes upward to look at the pockmarks on the ceiling tiles and took a deep breath. Tears pooled in the corners of my eyes anyway.

"It was bad," Polly said, "but I didn't know how bad either, really."

Daniel released her from his hug, and he held her shoulder with his good hand. Without taking my eyes off the ceiling, even though my tears were flowing freely again, I saw that they looked at each other for a long moment.

"Peej?" Daniel said. "I have to ask you a question, and I am sorry—"

"Daniel, no apologies," Polly said.

I looked down from the ceiling now.

"Uhm, okay." He let go of her shoulder and fumbled with the strap on his sling. He glanced out the window for a second and then back at Polly.

"Oh," Polly whispered.

"Yeah, when he, when Axel broke into your mom's place and…" Daniel looked over at me, and I nodded at him. Polly already knew. "P.J., he killed your mom. The phone kept recording the entire…the entire time."

"Oh," Polly said again. I moved to sit next to her on the bed. Polly pressed her fingertips to her head, right between her eyebrows. I put my arm around her, but she didn't collapse into me the way I expected her to. Her spine was as stiff as a steel girder.

"We have your cell phone at the precinct, you can have it. We took it from your apartment in case there was proof… evidence on it, and well, there is."

"I don't know," Polly said.

"No, okay," Daniel said, his eyes so soft on her. "We have a digital recording, so we can erase the message. We already have it. Your mother's…your mother's murder is already charged to Axel, even though he is dead."

Polly nodded.

"P.J.?" Daniel asked. Polly nodded again. Daniel's eyes met mine. "Why don't you call us in a few days to let us know if you want to hear the message or not. Some people think it's healing to…but I don't know."

Now Polly melted into my side. She turned her face to my neck, and I felt her shuddery exhalation against my skin.

"Thank you, Officer…Daniel," I said. I unwrapped one arm from Polly and held it out to him. He took my hand in his good one, and I squeezed all of my fear and all of my gratitude into his hand. "Thank you so much…for being there and for everything."

After he left, Polly pulled her face away from my neck. Without picking her head up off my shoulder, she asked me what I thought. I had to think a long time about that.

I knew it was a terrifying message, and I couldn't think of any reason Polly should listen to it. She had been through more than enough and I was wary of additional trauma. I decided to tell Polly what I saw in the last vision I had, the only one I had from which Polly was absent.

"Polly," I began, "Polly, I was there, kind of. I could see it..." She sat up, leaning away from me a bit, which hurt my heart, so she could see my face as I shared the story. I told her every detail of her mother's, of our mother's, death.

She listened without saying a word, her eyes glued to mine, until she closed them at the end of my vision. I could see faint bluish veins in her eyelids. I wondered if mine looked the same. In the end, Polly decided she didn't need to hear the recording, and that decision found me feeling very relieved. I could not bear to think of her listening to our mother's death.

We were quiet for a few hours. Nurses and the doctor came in to check on Polly, and then they left again. Asha came and went, making preparations for Polly to stay with us at the hotel until we decided it was time to get a flight home. Polly's friend, Kris, came to see Polly and cry with her.

After things quieted down I told Polly about my childhood, about the hole in my heart and especially about Guadalupe. Polly said she wished she could have met her. I wished so too. I told her about the people who had adopted me and raised me. I told her briefly of their crimes.

I didn't bore her with details I'd discovered over the past few days. I'd learned they were both still in custody and awaiting trial. My father had sold every material thing he owned, which was quite a bit, and had liquidated every other asset in his name in order to pay back some of what had been contributed to PDOC. He'd also written a public letter of apology in which he described falsifying the data for the fertility drug. This letter was published by many of the major newspapers. There were a few days when my parents' faces had been splashed all over the various forms of media. I couldn't avoid the news, even in this hospital in South Carolina. There was talk of a lawsuit coming my father's way from the pharmaceutical company, but he had told me over the phone that he wasn't worried about that since he still had proof of the bribe they used with him. He was worried, however, about his involvement in and knowledge of PDOC's transgressions.

Dr. Arthur Pinehurst had been pivotal in the FBI investigation. He was in no legal trouble since he had gotten out as soon as he knew things were amiss. I had a feeling, though, that he had been cut a deal because it seemed to me that he had kept this secret too long to not be considered culpable in some way.

I hadn't communicated at all with Margaret Windler. It was hard for me not to still consider them my mother and father, but such a large part of me was relieved that she was not my biological mother. I felt no connection to her even now, and I couldn't pretend to feel guilty or sad about that. These things, I kept to myself.

Polly and I had one last decision to make—our fourth of the day. Our mother's body was still downstairs in the hospital's refrigerator unit. She'd had to stay there until Polly was conscious and able to decide what to do with her remains. It was a long time to have a body chilled, but the hospital hadn't needed the unit, and the doctor had thought Polly would come to sooner than she had.

She decided to have our mother cremated, have a small memorial gathering at the shoreline near the carnival and scatter most of her ashes into the ocean. I let Polly make this decision because she knew best what our mother would have wanted. I suggested, however, that Polly and I keep a small container of our mother's ash so that we always had a part of her with us. I wasn't ready to give up my biological mother yet.

Polly cried again, and when she could, she told me that the ache in her heart was also for me, for my never having known our mother and for all that we had lost as twin children.

"What do you know," I asked, "of our separation?"

"You mean when it happened? The beginning?"

I nodded and chewed my bottom lip. I hoped this was fair to ask her. Polly looked down at her hands and then at me. I was staring at myself when I looked into her eyes.

She took a deep breath, and began. "One of us was already spoken for, even before we were born." She watched me carefully as she said the words.

"And the other one?" I asked.

Now she chewed her bottom lip. Was she worried about my reaction?

"Polly, it's okay. I'm okay with whatever you say. I just want to know the truth."

"The truth makes your parents—the Windlers, I mean— look bad."

"I'm okay with that," I said.

"If you're sure…" She waited for my nod and then continued. "One of us was spoken for, but the other one was a surprise. Dr. Windler and his wife arranged to buy her baby because Mom knew she couldn't give a child all it deserved." Polly's voice quavered and she swallowed hard. "Well, that's what she had decided when she first learned she was pregnant— that she wasn't enough, didn't have enough." Polly pressed her lips together. I reached out and took her hand in mine.

I waited. I smoothed the soft, tan skin on the back of her hand with my thumb, back and forth, back and forth until she could speak again.

"Anyway, when she was five months pregnant, she went for a checkup at Ocean View Memorial Hospital, and a doctor there knew of a couple in Minnesota who wanted to adopt a baby, but didn't want it to be public knowledge." Polly stopped and arched an eyebrow at me. I was frowning and nodding and hadn't even been aware of it until she'd looked at me like that.

"Of course they wanted a baby," I explained. "Lawrence Windler was the number one fertility doctor at the time. How could he and his wife *not* have a baby?" I felt a knot the size of a peach pit form in my stomach. My whole childhood had been a sham, hadn't it? I had been a trophy child, an emblem of their success with fertility. Now it was Polly's turn to pet the back of my hand.

"I'm sorry," she said. Her frown matched mine.

"What else?" I held back tears. They trickled down the back of my throat.

"Well, like I said, one of us surprised Mom." She smiled. "Oh, and there was no 'Dad.' Or no dad that Mom was ever able to tell me about. I think we are love children, but I don't think we'll ever know. But anyways…Mom has a…had a good memory for details. She told me when Dr. Windler and his wife and their nanny came to get their baby, that he offered to buy both of us, but his wife said absolutely not—that there'd be twice the screaming, twice the diapers, twice the coloring on the walls, twice the college tuition. Dr. Windler said then that it would be twice as good for his reputation, as if this might change his wife's mind, but she was dead set against two. She said…" Polly looked away from me.

"What? She said what?"

"She said one would be bad enough," Polly whispered, looking at my hand in hers. I couldn't answer her. We sat in silence for a few moments. The knot in my stomach tightened itself even more. I think had it not been for Polly's very bright orange and green pajamas, I would have been awash in self-pity. As it was, I looked at her sitting there cross-legged in front of me, holding my hand, and was enveloped in such a profound feeling of love and completeness that I couldn't be bothered to feel sorry for myself. The knot loosened slightly.

"I'm okay," I said.

"All right. So Mom knew she couldn't take a baby to the boardwalk while she was at work…she was a carny, like me…so she tried to talk Mrs. Windler into it as well, into taking both of us. The nanny, your Guadalupe, was already holding you in her arms. She was right next to the bassinette I was lying in, the one we'd shared, and when she walked away, apparently I howled, and that pissed your…Mrs. Windler off even more and she said one was enough. Dr. Windler didn't know how to choose. He asked if one was a boy, but no."

"Seriously? He asked for a boy?" I asked.

"Yeah, he did," Polly answered with a quiet voice.

I shook my head but couldn't say anything more about it.

Polly continued, "So his wife said the nanny could choose. That's when Mom started crying because she was scared about having to keep one of the babies, and then the nanny started crying too. She had finally realized what was happening."

That did make me cry. How could they have put Lupe in that situation? How could they? Having to make that decision must have scarred Lupe's soul. I wondered if her devotion had been to my family as I'd believed all along, or if it had all been solely for me because she knew what a hole I'd have in my heart without my twin. I took my hand from Polly's, covered my face and bawled.

"Cassie." Polly scooted closer to me and held me. How could they?

Tears fell into my lap. Polly patted my back and rocked me. Her head was pressed beside mine and I could hear one of our heartbeats. Or both of them beating in rhythm. The thought calmed me. I listened to our heartbeats. Okay. That had happened too long ago to cry about it now.

Then another thought struck me. What if Guadalupe had chosen Polly? I wouldn't have known her. I would have missed out on Guadalupe.

My tears erupted all over again. God, I was a mess. I tried to even out my breathing. In time my tears slowed too. I sniffled and Polly broke away for a minute, leaving my arms and back cold, but then she came in close again. A tissue appeared beneath my dripping nose. I chuckled into it. I sat up, blew my nose properly and smoothed back my hair.

"I'm sorry," I said to Polly.

"Oh my God, are you kidding me?" she gasped. "We have every right to be full-blown disasters right now. Complete basket cases. Every reason." She continued to rub little circles on my back.

"Well, you might as well tell me the rest, if there's more. My heart's already annihilated." I sniffled, smiled and blew my nose again.

"So the nanny, Guadalupe, couldn't take it. She walked out of the bedroom where the bassinette was, and I kept screaming—

probably for you—and the nanny started singing a song to you, even though she was still crying. Like I said, Mom had a pretty good memory for details. She sang the nanny's song to me every day when I was growing up. Later she told me she sang it because she didn't know how else to keep me and you connected. But I didn't know that then. I still don't know what the song means, even now, but it goes something like '*Santa, santa, colita de rana, si no santa hoy, santa mañana.*'"

Tears threatened again to hear the song Guadalupe had sung to me almost every day of my childhood. I laughed despite the need to cry. How was it that Polly had a good singing voice while I sounded like a strangling cat when I sang?

"That was Guadalupe's song," I said. "You kind of changed a word or two, but it was the song Lupe said her mother sang to her when she got a cut or a sliver as a child in Mexico. She said it made her happy to have someone to sing it to even though it made her miss her mother."

"Oh." Polly smiled

"Sing it again, but with the words, '*Sana, sana, colita de rana, si no sanas hoy, sanarás mañana.*' You have a nice singing voice." Polly sang it again, with the right words this time, and my heart ached. For a moment, we just looked at each other.

"Do you know what it means?" she finally asked.

"I do. It means, 'Heal, heal, little frog's tail. If you don't heal today, you'll heal tomorrow.' I guess it was pretty appropriate for her to sing as we were being separated."

"Yeah," Polly mused. She laughed and said, "You know how we're born on Leap Day?"

"Yeah?"

"Well, this song…the part about the little frog's tail…it kind of makes us leapfrogs then, doesn't it?"

"Yeah, it does, I guess," I said. That made me smile. Leaplings and frogs.

"Leapfrogs, that's what we are." Polly looked pleased with herself, and I was pretty impressed with her myself. Leapfrogs. It reminded me of another nickname I'd been given.

I told Polly, "You know, she used to call me '*Mi mitad de la Bodoquito*' and I never knew why. She told me it meant 'my half bundle' or something like that. Now, knowing you and our story, it makes sense."

"You were lucky to have her," Polly said. Her voice was so gentle.

Over the past few days, I'd tried to ignore the ripplings of jealousy that had surfaced. I felt guilt over the envy I felt when I thought about how fortunate Polly was to have known our mom. Whenever I'd tried to think of her as *our* mom, I added in my heart, *well, really, Polly's mom*. But hearing Polly say now that I was lucky to have had Lupe, I realized she was right. I was right too, but I didn't need to rationalize or measure and compare our luck—we were both fortunate. Polly hadn't had the same material advantages that I'd had. Then again she didn't have to feel guilty about having benefitted from charity and pharmaceutical fraud.

"You were lucky too," I told her, hoping she knew what I meant.

"I know," she answered. She smiled at me with sadness in her eyes.

"*We* are lucky." I smiled back, trying to keep any grief out of my own eyes. My heart was actually beginning to feel lighter again.

"Do you know who we are named for?" Polly asked.

"Well, I was named after Cassandra, my father's mother. They just decided to shorten it to Cassie."

"Hm." Polly didn't look convinced. She narrowed her eyes at me and smiled like the Mona Lisa.

"What?"

"Our mom named you Cassie," she said.

"Really?" A huge grin split across my face. My mom, my real mom, had named me? My heart pressed at my ribcage. "Did she really?"

"Yes, and I'm Polly. Like Castor and Pollux? You know?"

"The Gemini twins? They're boys, or men, or whatever. And they didn't have happy endings."

"Well, they wound up as stars in the sky, so that's kind of nice. Mom was a big reader. She loved mythology more than any other type of story," Polly explained.

"You're a big reader too," I said.

"Yeah, I can't help it." She ducked her head and smiled at me.

"Hey," she said, "want to know how much you cost?" She lifted her eyebrows twice, devilishly.

I thought about it. I was sitting here with my sister, with my twin. A few weeks ago I hadn't even know she'd existed, really. My heart was full of both realities and of memories. It had been crushed by Guadalupe's death, chewed up by my parents, and spat out by Axel. But at the same time, it was wonderfully intact. I didn't need to know anything else right now.

I laughed out loud. "No, I do *not* want to know how much I cost."

"Okay, but let's just say you were quite a bargain. Mom had to keep using the library because she still couldn't afford to buy her own books."

Both of the visions I'd had of our mother were still sharp in my mind, one being the vision of her comforting Polly as she let her know she wasn't alone in this world and the other being of her murder. Even though they were both laced with sorrow, I knew that these visions were gifts to me. I didn't know whom to thank for those visions, so I thanked Fate for allowing me to have this life that was finally unfolding. I also sent out silent thanks for the dinner conversation I'd had with Linda Crespo. Without hearing about her studies on twin communication, I probably would never have realized exactly what was going on between Polly and me.

I wondered if there was much research on telepathy between mothers and their children. Probably not, unlike the amount of research on twins. I decided that this was going to be my next topic of study. I figured I had nothing to lose. All I had was a great deal more about my own experience to understand. But that would all come much later. For now, all I wanted to do was get to know my sister and continue to get to know my sweet fiancée.

CHAPTER THIRTY

Annie's Ashes

My hair lashed out in all directions. It whipped across my eyes, making them sting, but as I was already crying, it didn't matter. For appearance's sake, I tugged the hood of my jacket up over my head and tried to arrest the unruly tresses, tucking them back as far as I could into the hood. Asha's hair looked perfect. It was too short to get ruffled by this strong coastal breeze. Polly's hair, however, was as wild as mine. She didn't seem to mind.

Polly's doctor had advised against attempting even moderate activity so soon, but Polly wasn't going to listen. I kept my eyes on her for any evidence of exhaustion or frailty, but she seemed to be lit from within. She glowed. Her eyes were clear and bright green, her cheeks held healthy color, and even the bruising at the left side of her face was barely detectable unless the wind lifted her hair over her ear to reveal her stitches. I hoped it wasn't adrenaline that was giving her this boost, that she really was on the mend.

"Over here," Polly called out to us. She picked her way along the rocks at the ocean's edge, carrying the deep blue ceramic vase that held our mother's ashes—save for the two little shares we had each kept for ourselves. The ashes were secured in a plastic bag inside the vase, thank goodness; otherwise, the wind would have already made short work of our mission here. The small memorial party followed Polly's beckoning.

"You okay?" Asha said just loudly enough for me to hear over the wind. She put her arm through mine as we came up to the place Polly had chosen.

"Yes, I think so," I answered. Asha's black eyes sparkled as she scrutinized my face for any signs that I wasn't being truthful. "I am," I reassured her. I squeezed her arm in mine.

We were a group of nine, ten if I counted our mother's spirit, on the Atlantic shore. The sun was about to set behind us, and the jaunty music of the boardwalk amusement park sounded far, far off, even though it was little more than a stone's throw away, by Polly's measurement, from where we stood. She must have a good arm, I thought. I smiled to myself. She would have a good arm from slamming closed and yanking open hundreds, maybe even hundreds of thousands of Tilt-A-Whirl safety bars over the course of her life. That and hoisting all those heavy classical paperback books.

"Okay, then," Polly said. She turned to face us. "I guess this is it."

"This is perfect, Peej," Kris said as she came up and stood before Polly. I'd met her already, albeit informally, or would it be surreally? I'd seen her in the very first vision I'd had of Polly. Kris was the woman who'd sat beside Polly at Sandy's bar, the woman Polly had kissed on the cheek as she was getting ready to leave. She was Polly's best friend.

"It is," Sandy agreed. The rest of us nodded our consent and waited for Polly to continue.

Four of our mother's friends, Roger, Clay, Dora and Trudy, were gathered in a semicircle facing the ocean and facing Polly, beside Kris, Sandy, Asha and me. The love and grief were tangible, and even if the wind hadn't been responsible for our watering eyes, I knew when we'd gathered up outside the Sand Bar to walk together to the ocean that none of us were going to stop crying. The waves crashing and angry behind Polly provided a stark contrast to Polly's gentle energy. Her face, so delicate and serene, was lit up in a warm golden wash from the sinking sun as she looked at us. Her lips were pressed together now, and I wondered if she'd be able to do this.

"I am so thankful…" Polly began, but she had to stop. She opened her eyes wide, looked up at the sky and then back down at us. She wore no mascara, and her eyelashes glinted coppery in the fading light. She let out a long, deep shuddery sigh, and I watched her face crumple. Her serenity was replaced by a mournful sadness. Her renewed crying brought out answering sniffles and quiet sobs from the rest of us. After a short time, Polly smiled through her heartache and tears, though, and I knew she'd be fine.

"I am so thankful that you are all…no," she paused. "Cassie?"

She held out the hand that wasn't holding our mother's ashes. I left the group to go stand beside her. The wind died abruptly as I took the two or three steps to her. She took my hand in hers. "*We* are so happy and thankful that you were our mother's friends and that you are here now to help us say good-bye to her."

Polly spoke of our mother, of her dreams, of her passions and of her sacrifices. Every face looking back at us was intent on Polly's words. The absence of the wind seemed a sign of respect that the world held for our mother. I could sense without even turning around that the waves at our backs had grown gentler.

It was the second memorial I'd been to in a very short time. The second "mother's" memorial. Guadalupe had been the truest mother I'd had, and now she was gone. Annie Flynn had been my biological mother that I hadn't even been aware of and now she was also gone—before I could even properly meet her. The woman who'd pretended to be my mother, Margaret Windler, was essentially gone too, being held in a low-security women's prison until her trial concluded. Truth be told, I mourned the loss of Guadalupe Hermila Delgado Lagunas and

Annie Flynn much more than I mourned Margaret Windler's absence. How many mothers could a person have? I seemed to have both a dearth and an overabundance at this point.

"I remember the day my mother, our mother, told me I had a sister—and a twin no less!" Polly recounted. She squeezed my hand. I remembered that day too; I had envisioned a part of that conversation, hadn't I?

"I felt both elated," Polly went on, "and crushed because I had known, I had known, for my whole life before that, that I was missing a part of me, that I wasn't alone, but…" She turned her head to meet my gaze. I was looking in the mirror. Her need for me matched my need for her, and it was apparent on her face. She nodded and smiled. I smiled back.

"Annie Flynn has left behind the greatest gift any mother could," Polly said. "She left me my other half."

There were a few minutes of silence during which the sun decided to make her graceful exit behind the buildings on the coast. Now we were all cast in a balmy pink hue. Eventually Annie and Polly's friends each shared their favorite memories of Annie with the group. With the telling of every tale, my heart ached more for not having known her. The stories made us laugh and cry, and I realized she had been an amazingly warm and genuine person.

By the time we were ready to release Annie to the wind and water, the only lights were the carnival lights of the boardwalk. The pink tones of earlier had been replaced by myriad colors from the various rides and vendors' booths. The piping tunes of the carnival melded with the gentle thunder of the waves, which were growing larger again.

Polly held the vase between her knees as she undid the twisty-tie at the top of the plastic bag. She folded the bag down over the top of the vase and held our mother's ashes out to each of us. We each scooped up a handful. Sandy ran then, up the beach, stooping and sprinkling bits of Annie Flynn into the rolling tide as she went. Roger, Dora and Asha followed her. Sandy and Dora were whooping their good-byes into the returning breeze. Kris, Clay and Trudy stood still as they let Annie Flynn's ashes sift through their fingers into the ocean at their feet.

I held my mother's ashes in my hand for a long time, as did Polly. I looped my arm through hers and we walked down the beach and into the wind until we were alone. The ashes in my hand were warm now. I was reluctant to let them go. The wind was picking up, and our hair was lifted and messed by it. I looked at Polly, and we laughed and cried.

"Okay?" I asked her.

She nodded.

Without speaking, we tossed our mother's ashes high into the wind, letting the strong breeze carry them back onto us. I didn't close my eyes. I couldn't bring myself to do so for fear of missing one more moment with my real mother. The ashes drifted like stardust over us, covering us in a fine film of mother, of Annie Flynn. I licked my lips. Her grit was now a part of me, I guessed. I smiled, and I knew from looking at Polly that she had done the same, and I knew that I had twin tear tracks running down my cheeks that were identical to hers. Still holding the vase in one arm, Polly hugged me hard to her, pressing our mother's ashes into the fibers of our jackets, before we joined the rest of the memorial party.

That night, Polly slept in her bed in the hotel room, as Asha and I slept in ours. It was our last night there in Myrtle Beach. Tomorrow we'd board the plane that would carry us to the rest of our lives. I knew what my life had in store for me, and I so looked forward to it. I wondered as I began to fall asleep whether Polly looked forward to what was ahead for her. She'd never traveled out of South Carolina. Was she scared? I didn't think so. I felt sleep taking over, and I gave in. Neither Polly nor I had showered before going to bed. We slept embraced in our mother's ashes.

CHAPTER THIRTY-ONE

The Fertility Thief's Daughter

"PDOC Pirate," blared the headline above the photo of Margaret Windler's steely face.

"Fertility Thief" was emblazoned above the gentle countenance of my father.

"Oh my god," Asha said. She bent over to peer at the headlines and then read the finer print as we stood before the newsstand at the Minneapolis-St. Paul International Airport. "Oh my god!" she repeated.

I leaned over next to her to get a better look, and my backpack, which I'd only slung over one shoulder, fell off me and thumped onto the floor.

"Wow…" I said. My heart raced to see my parents on the front page of one of the national newspapers. I grabbed one strap of my backpack and straightened up.

"Who's that?" Polly asked, even though it looked like she didn't really want to know the answer.

"Pol, meet my parents, the Windlers," I said with a gentle hand flourish in the direction of the newspaper. Why couldn't it have been a tabloid? Why the *Wall Street Journal*?

"Oh yeah," she said. She leaned forward to see them. "You'd told me about this. Wow." She stood up, and so did Asha. "I'm sorry, Cassie," Polly said.

"This says your dad is going to plead guilty. They're both still awaiting trial," Asha said.

Her eyebrows were drawn together. She seemed to be waiting for my reaction. I had none. I felt cold. I had expected this…Well, not the newspaper but I had expected that they'd be convicted of their respective crimes. "PDOC pirate"? That was clever, but "fertility thief"? My heart hurt to read that one. My father, the fertility thief.

I thought about it the whole way home and then, after getting Asha and Polly settled, the whole way to the university. It couldn't be argued, could it? He had stolen many people's fertility, hadn't he? I would never be able to understand why he did what he'd done, but I couldn't bring myself to judge him, for some reason. My mother…no, Margaret Windler, *her* I could judge, no problem. Why was that? Was it because she kept at her abuse and misuse of the PDOC funds whereas my father had committed his crime once and long ago? Was it because I saw her as the impetus for my father's crime? I wasn't sure.

I let myself into my office, flipped on the light and flopped into the chair behind my desk, which was in relatively good order except for an overflowing in-box. I wondered how Asha and Polly were faring. It was Asha who had prompted me to come to the university today, even though she wasn't returning to work until tomorrow. She'd been able to conduct most of her business over the phone and computer, and I'd had my graduate assistant step into my place during my absence, so neither of us had had to worry much, but it did feel good, normal, to be here. I'd only been gone for seven school days, but it felt like it had been longer.

There was a tapping outside my office door, and I spun in my chair to see Arthur Pinehurst standing, his face open in question, waiting for me to invite him in. I did, and he sat down on the empty chair. He ran his hand through his unruly hair. I watched and smiled when, as usual, it sprang back to where it had been before he'd tried to tame it.

"Welcome back," he said.

"Thank you, Art."

"Do you hate me?" His question caught me off guard. I felt the same feeling I'd felt earlier staring at my father's eyes on the front of the newspaper. My heart tensed uncomfortably. His question made me feel his vulnerability, and that hurt me.

"Hate you?"

"Yes, Cassie, hate me. For the part I played in the investigation."

"Oh." Did I? Not at all. "No, Art, I don't."

"It would be understandable if you did," he said. His eyes searched my face from beneath his crazy thick eyebrows. "I started things, by coming clean to the FBI. I went to them, Cassie. They didn't come to me." He looked at me. "I need you to know that."

I took off my glasses and rubbed my forehead between my eyebrows. I had not known that. He was responsible for my parents' fate? He had caused all of this?

"Art, you only played a part in the pharmaceutical research, not PDOC. What happened there?"

"The FBI was already looking into that—that wasn't me. But with your father...that...that was me." He swallowed hard but didn't take his eyes from mine. I was the one who had to look away. I studied the Hello Kitty picture Asha had colored for me. I scrutinized the books and papers stacked and shelved around the room. When there was nothing else to stare at, I dragged my eyes back to his. I couldn't be mad at him. He had every right to clear his conscience, didn't he?

"The papers are calling him the 'fertility thief,'" I said. My voice was quiet.

"I know. I am sorry, Cassie," he responded.

"You had to do what you had to do." I'd never used that tired, old cliché before, but nothing else fit. "And his involvement with PDOC is probably what's going to get him into the most trouble, not the fertility drug thing."

"I know, but I'm still sorry," Art repeated.

His forehead was a map of worry, his eyes were on mine and his mouth held in a slight frown. He looked at me the way my father had looked at me so often while I was growing up. I'd seen that same expression every time my mother, Margaret Windler, had done something petty or hateful to me. Every time she'd wheedled me into being her poster child, every time she cajoled me into believing she and my father really did have business to attend to at the same time I needed them, every time she had cut me out of her life, I'd seen that look on my father's face.

"You know, Cassie," Art said, "I'd gone to the police and they pushed me in the FBI's direction a few months before I'd started again at the university." He cleared his throat. "I had already started the ball rolling by the time I'd met you, and I…" He took a deep breath.

"Art, you don't have to—"

"No, I'm not apologizing because…well, I am, but this is in addition to my other apologies, I guess." He cleared his throat again. "When I met you, I liked you, right away. I *liked* you. I still like you. If I'd ever had a daughter, I'd have wanted her to be like you. And I'd wished then that I'd never talked to the FBI, that I'd never spoken a word of this to anyone, ever."

"Art," I said because I didn't know what else to say.

"But it was too late," he continued. He patted my forearm. "It was too late."

We were quiet then, for a long time. I leaned back in my chair and thought about his words. He had no children, I knew. I was touched, and I sensed he was speaking his truth, not just placating me so that I wouldn't hold a grudge. He was being honest with me. I felt Art would be a steady, firm presence in my life from here on out, and I was glad of it. He deserved my honesty in return for his.

"Art, it's never too late," I said, "and I have to tell you, well, I don't know how to say it, really…but a small part of me is happy…no, not happy, exactly. Relieved, I guess." He nodded at me so that I'd continue. "I knew somehow, all my life, I think, that something was amiss in my family—with the Windlers."

"I had wondered if maybe…" He let his words die out, unspoken.

"I did, all along," I said. "And now, now I feel relived to have the shoe drop, you know? To know for sure and to have had the worst happen. And to live through it."

I wasn't explaining myself well because I'd not taken the time to think about my feelings, but I attempted to share them with Art anyway because I felt he'd understand even if I did express myself badly. He nodded and patted my forearm again.

"Well, I am here for you, Cassie, and not out of guilt, but because I care about you, and I want the best for you."

"Thank you."

"You know, we may both find ourselves suffering some backlash from all this. Me as a whistleblower and you as a Windler," Art said.

I didn't say anything to that. I hadn't thought of any fallout that might come from being related—theoretically speaking, now—to a man who faked his research. Now that I did think of it, it wasn't anything I looked forward to; that was for certain.

Art continued, "So when you need to talk, I will listen, and if you have questions, I will find the answers, if I can, okay? We can stick together."

"Thank you, Art," I said. I smiled at him as he rose to leave my office.

"And, Cassie, we have missed you around here. Michael told me about your sister, and I am very happy about that, and I am sorry about your biological mother. Michael told me that too." He looked sheepish then. "I hope you don't mind. I was worried, so I kept pestering him for updates, and I think he told me everything just to get me off his back." I laughed picturing Art pestering Michael, and he looked relieved.

"Thank you, Art, I am glad he told you everything," I said, still chuckling. My heart had lightened, thinking of Polly, and I was surprised to feel a reluctant, hesitant joy at the thought of Annie Flynn. The memorial service had helped me come to terms, I thought, with the loss of my potential to ever really know her.

Art left, and I was alone with my thoughts for the first time in over a week. I spun lazily in my chair, swirling to the right, to the left and then back to the right.

I thought about what Art had shared and how he'd looked so much like my father during our conversation. He'd been apologetic and ready to listen. I was fortunate, wasn't I? I took a deep breath and thanked Fate again, this time for sending me a father figure when my own, Lawrence Windler, was indisposed. Funny how people show up when others are taken from you. Would it always be this way?

CHAPTER THIRTY-TWO

I Do...I Do, I Do, I Do, I Do, I Do

Running this morning felt like stepping into the mouth of a dragon. I kept asking the dragon to provide a little puff of fire to dry the air out, but the dragon just laughed in great, hot, steamy gusts of breath that threatened to blast me off his asphalt tongue. The unseasonable heat and humidity had not only encouraged the lilacs to burst into radiant life, but had brought scores of runners and dog walkers out of the woodwork. I dodged around and darted between the sidewalk traffic with a huge grin on my face. I was going to be illegally wed today to the love of my life.

After I got home and showered, which seemed rather pointless with the air's moisture level as high as it was, Asha called out to me from the kitchen that there was a letter from my father. I threw on a bikini top and a pair of cutoffs and padded downstairs in my bare feet.

"Maybe a wedding card?" she asked as she handed the envelope to me.

"Maybe," I said. I opened it up. It was indeed a wedding card and there was a letter inside.

Dear Cassie,

I have to begin by saying that I apologize more deeply to you than to anyone else in this world. When I adopted you from your biological mother, I thought I would do so much better by you than I have in actuality done. You deserved much more. I know your childhood was filled with a lack of attention from me and with a lack of affection from your mother, Margaret, and I wish it could have been different. I thank God for Guadalupe. I know she loved you very much. I hope you can forgive me someday.

I want to wish you and Asha all the love and joy that this world has to offer. I wish that I could be with you both on your very special day. I hope you know that in my heart I will be. I wish that I could walk you down the proverbial aisle, if you would still have me do so. There are some loves in this world that are very pure, loves that will not ever demand that laws be broken or people be trampled, and I am so grateful that you know that pure love with Asha. I am so thankful for that, Cassie.

You say you are not mad at me, but I know that you must have some anger or resentment inside of you for the things I have done and the things I have allowed to happen around me. I have lived in shame and in fear for most of my adult life, and now that everything is out in the open, I feel I am finally really, truly living. I feel I was "mostly dead" until now, to use a line from *The Princess Bride*, one of your favorite childhood movies. I do not blame Margaret. I can only blame myself. So if you do indeed have anger that is directed at me, know that I share this anger with you. I understand.

Any anger you do have toward me is justified. But, if you also find yourself pitying me, let me tell you, and please believe me, that there is no need for pity. As I wrote above, I finally feel fully alive. And even though I am here and not in charge of making more than one or two minor decisions a day, I feel freer than I ever have before. Let me repeat that to you, Cassie. I feel freer than I ever have before. I don't know how to explain it, but there it is.

All my love to you,
Your father,
Lawrence Windler

I decided that I was lucky to have had this man in my life after all, even if he wasn't my real father and even if he had forfeited his integrity for a woman he loved. He wanted happiness for me, and he loved me. I had known that, but the words in his letter reminded me. I handed Asha the letter and waited until she had read his words too.

"Well, Cass, my soon-to-be-wife, I can think of worse fathers-in-law a person could have," she said, handing me the letter and wrapping her arms around me from behind. She hung her head over my shoulder and placed her cheek alongside mine.

"He didn't do the best he could," I said, "but he is still a good man, I think." I set the letter on the countertop and tried to embrace Asha behind me in a sort of backward hug. I wound up with her buttocks in my hands. We laughed, but I didn't let go.

"I think so too," Asha agreed.

"And then there's Margaret Windler…you put up with her so well," I said.

"No," I could feel her shaking her head, "not anymore. Once we discovered she's not your real mom…no. To be honest, I'm glad she's not going to be one of my in-laws. Your dad is okay, but not Margaret."

"She's more of your out-law now, anyway, than an in-law," I added. Asha chuckled.

"You know, she probably did the best she could with what she had…we shouldn't be too hard on her," Asha conceded.

"You always think the best of people," I reminded her.

"I know; can't help it." She released her grip from around my shoulders and let her fingertips graze me from the low waistline of my shorts to the bottom of my ribcage and back down. I leaned back into her and copied her movements on the southern side of her buttocks. Through the thin fabric of her pajama pants I could feel that I had brought out goosebumps on her skin. Ahh, delicious.

Polly rounded the corner of the kitchen doorway just then, took one look at us and headed back out just as quickly as she'd almost come in.

"Oh my god, you lovebirds!" she drawled. "I am so sorry to interrupt!" I could hear her laughing her way into the living room.

"Don't be," Asha called out to her. "The kitchen is now all yours! And the coffee is ready!" She dragged me by the hand out of the kitchen and back up the stairs to our bedroom.

She led me over to the bed, gently shoved me down on the duvet and crossed the room again to quietly shut the door. She leaned back against the closed door, crossed her arms over her chest and looked at me on the bed. She had a sexy little smirk on her face, and she nodded approvingly.

"This is my last chance to make love to an unmarried woman," she said, cocking one eyebrow. "Better make the most of it, eh?"

* * *

Three hours later we were scrambling around the room, my hair still damp from showering, Asha's sticking out in all directions from leaving the towel on her head for too long as she began the search for her cummerbund. A cummerbund. Yes, the woman I was marrying was going to sport a cummerbund at our ceremony. Her hair towel had fallen on my satin shoes, so now I was waving the left one around in the air to dry the water it had absorbed from the towel. I gave up; it was too humid to worry about it now. If the spot dried, it dried, if not, so be it.

A knock at the door was followed by Polly's head peeking into the room.

"May I come in?" she asked.

"Yes, let's see you!" Asha stopped the cummerbund search and opened the door to reveal Polly in a brilliant blue dress that matched the cut of the white dress I was wearing. She was breathtaking. Her copper hair hung below her shoulders, the same as mine, and she looked so happy as she spun for us, sending the hem of the knee-length dress in a lazy, wide arc. The dress dipped almost indecently low in the back, and it fit her perfectly.

"You look beautiful, just beautiful, and so happy," she said to me. She clapped her hands in front of her before rushing to me to give me a hug.

"Look at you two," Asha beamed. "Salt and pepper shakers."

"Yeah," I laughed. It still gave me a start to see Polly around the house. It was like coming across a mirror that you didn't know was hung there. She looked just like me. Or I looked just like her. She had lost the worry lines on her forehead, and her face was not drawn the way it had been in my visions of her. It goes to show how physically aging stress can be, I thought.

"Oh no!" Polly yelped in the southeast accent that still cracked me up. "You two are not supposed to see each other before the ceremony!"

"Well, I'd better get out of here then," I said, putting the satin shoes on my feet and standing up to leave Asha with a few moments' peace. When I straightened up and flipped my hair back over my shoulder, Asha was looking at me with such candid love in her eyes that I had to hightail it out of there before I ruined my mascara with tears.

* * *

The ceremony was perfect. Asha and I had decided to have a circle ceremony so that we weren't plunked down in front of everyone, but rather so that we were part of the circle. Just four days prior, to the surprise and pleasure of so many, Minnesota's governor had signed the same-sex marriage bill. We'd be having a small, legal wedding sometime after August first when the marriage certificates would be available. But for this ceremony, Michael was our unordained priest. Neither Asha nor I felt the need to worry about the religious aspect, and since this wasn't our legal marriage, we didn't have to get hung up on the paperwork either. We had Michael officiate, not because we thought a guy should perform the ceremony, but because he volunteered before we had even thought of who might do the ceremony, and we'd decided he was the perfect person when we'd had a chance to discuss it.

Esme sang two songs from the islands, and there was not a dry eye in the backyard by the time she finished. After the formal part was over, the drinking, dining and dancing began. I introduced Whitney to my new sister, and she introduced her new daughter and her daughter's partner to me. Both were lovely and friendly, and I'll be damned if Whitney's daughter wasn't the spitting image of her! Had they run into each other by accident they would have been dumbfounded. Lookalikes seemed to be the theme tonight.

"Ohhh, *la marasa*, she is your twin!" Esme said, her eyes wide in amazement as she looked at Polly and me standing next to each other. Esme had been visiting relatives in the islands since mid-March and hadn't yet met Polly. "I didn't get a good look from where I was in the circle, but *mon dieu*, now I see the two of you here. How is it you didn't know, *chouchou*?" Sandy the bartender and Polly's best friend Kris had flown out for the wedding. They stood beside Esme with their faces echoing the wonderment behind Esme's question.

"I did know, Es," I said. "I mean, I kind of knew, somehow…" My voice trailed off, and I decided to let it go for now. Kris nodded at my answer, which was really a nonanswer. She grabbed Polly's hand, kissed it and pressed it to her own heart. Did it matter if I couldn't explain it? Not really. The people who loved us understood, even if they didn't really understand. It's not like I was going to have to write some scientific report on this or give some highfalutin presentation tonight about twin vision, or "twinsight," as I had started calling what I'd experienced. I could, now, speak from a place of experience on the whole matter, and the research part could come later.

I thought of Linda Crespo from the botched San Diego conference trip. On second thought, that trip wasn't really botched, was it? Would I have put two and two together without having heard Linda's twin telepathy theories? I looked beyond our small group toward the patio table where the remainder of our mother's ashes rested in two tiny identical blue silk pouches tucked inside a conch shell. No, I probably would not have put it all together. I'd still be wondering what the heck all these visions were, and, I thought with a bolt of fear, the visions would have stopped coming, wouldn't they? If Fate had taken Axel's side, my other half, *mi bodoquito*, would have been erased from this world. I would have to send Linda a huge thank-you email someday. But for now, I decided I was simply going to enjoy the experience rather than study it.

I also wanted to send Guadalupe a huge thank you for giving me my sister. Without her letter, I never would have been certain. I wouldn't have been complete. I toyed with the tiny scrap of red ribbon that was sewn into the bodice of my dress, right between my breasts, and smiled up into the evening sky. *Thank you, Guadalupe, thank you.*

As things began to wind down late that night, Asha and I stood close together, barely moving to the music, in the middle of the backyard. Most of the wedding-goers had gone home already, and the ones who were there were grouped up in twos and threes drinking and chatting on patio chairs. I noted that Michael had not left Polly's side for more than two minutes the entire night. His relationship with Melinda had fizzled out shortly after the spring semester began. Nothing had gone wrong, he said, but there was just a very limited supply of chemistry, and when they had used it up, there was no hope of getting more. I had thought it a pity because she seemed like a good person, but now I had to reconsider. Michael and Polly had danced and dined the night away with each other, and now they were cozied up on the wooden swing.

"Did I ever tell you that my last girlfriend did not marry me?" Asha asked me, with her lips pressed close to my cheekbone. I leaned back in her arms to look at her. She was glowing. She was absolutely perfect. I smiled. I didn't have a clever response ready this time. Asha waited for my reply. I had nothing.

"It's true," she filled in the silence. "It's true, so that's why I had to come looking for you." All I could do was try to contain the welling in my heart and kiss Asha's laughing mouth. She won that one.

Bella Books, Inc.

Women. Books. Even Better Together.

P.O. Box 10543
Tallahassee, FL 32302

Phone: 800-729-4992
www.bellabooks.com